S'mores

Book Three of the Brady Boe Series

By Taunya S. Wright

Nashville TN

Publisher: MAWMedia Group

First Edition: March 2016

S'mores Book Three of the Brady Boe Series/By Taunya S. Wright

ISBN: 978-1-943616-14-5

MAWMedia Group, LLC
2525 Somerset Drive
Nashville, TN 37217

www.mawmedia.com

DEDICATION

I would like to dedicate this book to every young girl that struggles with who she is. Understanding who you are begins with valuing and accepting yourself inside and out.

Taunya S. Wright

Table of Contents

Prologue

What a school year! Brady Boe had come out of her shell long enough to make new friends. Margie was thoughtful. Terra was a know it all. Ryan had grown on her. He could be just plain annoying at times, but sometimes he was somewhat funny. Then, there was Mrs. Ramsey, Brady Boe's teacher. He thought Brady Boe was special. She appreciated Mrs. Ramsey, but she just did not know how to say it without sounding silly. Sasha her sister, on the other hand, had no problem sounding or looking silly. She just did whatever she was feeling. Brady Boe envied this about Sasha. It was still hard for Brady Boe to deal with all her emotions. It seemed like she wanted to laugh, cry, and be upset all at the same time. Petunia, her mom, reminded her that each of these challenges was a part of growing up.

The best part of the school year was making the newspapers. Everyone in her class wanted one. She was popular for a season. It was one of those rare moments. She felt normal like other kids. No one looked at her as if she did not belong. Brady Boe could not let Petunia know how out of place she felt sometimes. She did not want her to worry or think she was unhappy.

The black car Brady Boe and Sasha saw on their way home from school peaked her curiosity. Brady Boe had her suspicions. It made her parents worry too. None of this happened until after Iona died. Brady Boe entertained the idea that her birth mom really wanted her. Brady Boe knew that, one day, her birth mom would answer all of her questions about why she gave her up. Her identity was hanging in limbo. She had to know the reasons. She felt it was the only way to find herself, whoever she was.

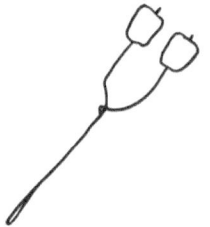

Chapter 1
Camp Anyone?

Today was it! Brady Boe would ask her parents about going to camp. She had not heard from Terra and Margie yet, but she was sure Terra was going. Margie, she was not so sure. She was not even sure if she was going to be able to go. It had been two weeks since school let out. Brady Boe, Sasha Brady Boe's little sister, and Taylor—a friend who lived across the street—had been swimming at least two times at the neighborhood pool. The temperature seemed to be hotter than usual for a Nashville summer. Petunia made sure there was plenty of lemonade in the refrigerator at all times. Brady Boe's father Mike could easily drink a whole pitcher by himself. Brady Boe could hear Sasha and Marcus playing in the living room as she lie in the bed contemplating whether to get up. Would she start her day, or ignore the bright light shining through her window inviting her to come outside? The printout that Terra gave her about camp still lay on her desk. She finally convinced herself to roll out of bed, and look at it.

Sasha came charging into Brady Boe's room just as Brady Boe picked up the paper. Marcus was right behind her growling like a monster.

"Brady Boe, save me!" yelled Sasha.

Brady Boe grabbed Marcus, placed him on the floor, and tickled him until he almost cried. When she let him go, he scrambled to his feet and dashed out of her room as fast as he could.

"Thanks, Brady Boe, for saving me from the monster." Brady Boe smiled. She had an idea. "Why are you smiling like that?" asked Sasha. She knew Brady Boe was up to something. She had seen that smile before.

Brady Boe handed Sasha the paper. "Being the big sister and all, and then saving you from Marcus, I think you owe me a favor."

"Oh, I remember this Brady Boe. Are we going to be able to go?"

"I don't know, Sasha. That's what I need you to find out today."

"Why me? I always ask. You do it this time."

"Alright, Sasha. You're not going to make this easy are you? We'll ask together. Do you still want to go?"

"Yes! Of course I do. It will be so much fun, Brady Boe. Let's go ask mom now. She's outside in the back."

"Hold on, Sasha. I have to prepare myself." Sasha was already pulling her out of the room.

Petunia was picking lemons. Mike was holding the basket. Their conversation captivated them so much that they did not see or hear the girls come outside. Sasha cleared her throat loudly.

Petunia and Mike turned their attention to the girls, surprised to see them standing in front of them. "When did you two get here?" asked Petunia.

"I don't know what you two are up to, but you want something," said Mike.

Both Brady Boe and Sasha continued to grin like twin Cheshire cats. After a couple of seconds, Brady Boe nudged Sasha with her elbow. Sasha took her cue, and spoke up.

"We were wondering, if you ever decided whether or not we could go to camp this summer?"

Brady Boe extended her arm with the paper in hand. Mike and Petunia glanced at each as if neither of them had ever heard about what the girls were describing. Brady Boe hated when that happened, because she would now have to plead her case all over again. Petunia stepped carefully off the ladder. Mike sat the basket of lemons down on the ground, and took the paper from Brady Boe. After reading the information quickly, he handed the paper to Petunia. Petunia looked it over briefly.

"Oh I remember this. Sorry, girls. I forgot all about it. Your dad and I will have to discuss it. Camp Firefly. I believe this is the same camp Taylor's mom mentioned Taylor would be going to this summer."

"Taylor is going too. Can we pleassse go mommy? It will be so much fun! Begged Sasha.

Brady Boe did not dare stop her either. This was the perfect time for her little sister to be dramatic.

"Brady Boe, didn't you mention you had some friends from school that were going?"

Brady Boe still wore her silly grin, "Yes. Margie and Terra. Terra has gone before. She said it was a lot of fun."

"Well, you know this is a stay over camp. Your dad and I will have to give it some thought."

Mike patted Brady Boe and Sasha on the head. "I'm off to work. We will discuss it when I get home. In the meantime, you girls think about what we would expect of you if we allowed you to stay at camp for a week." He kissed Petunia before leaving. Brady Boe pulled Sasha's arm.

"Let's go, Sasha. We have to make a list!"

"What are you talking about Brady Boe… a list of what?"

"Didn't you hear what dad said? He wants us to think about what they expect out of us. Sasha, this is our opportunity to help them not worry about us at camp. Think about how much fun we are going to have."

Sasha looked off in the distance for a moment. She thought about all the campfires and fun she would have with Taylor and her sister.

"Earth to Sasha! You really don't have all day to daydream, Sasha. We have work to do."

Sasha snapped out of her dream world and followed quickly behind Brady Boe. Once they were back in Brady Boe's room, Brady Boe took a piece of paper from her desk and plopped down on her bed. Sasha joined her eager and ready to help.

"We are going to make a list Sasha of everything that will put our parents' minds at ease."

Sasha raised her hand. "I got something."

"Why are you raising your hand Sasha? You're not in school. Just say it."

"We can tell them we are going to stay together all the time. They always say for us to do that anyways."

"Good one, Sasha. We'll keep writing until we fill up this paper."

Brady Boe and Sasha worked on their list throughout the day. Petunia told them they had to take a break for lunch. Marcus refused to be ignored. He came in Brady Boe's room several times to remind them of what having a baby brother is all about. He jumped on Sasha's back. He took Brady Boe's pencil whenever she put it down. The girls would give in and play with him for a little while. Then, they would get back to work. When the girls finally finished putting all they could think of on the list, they sat in the living room waiting anxiously for Mike to come home. Petunia was in the kitchen starting dinner. Marcus was watching one of his favorite cartoons in the kitchen breakfast area.

The door opened, and both Brady Boe and Sasha jumped from their seats. Sasha was the first to leap into Mike's arms. "Daddy, it took forever for you to get home!"

Mike gave Petunia a look. Brady Boe knew her mom would tell him all about how anxious she and Sasha were about going to camp, and how they worked on the assigned list all day.

"Well, now that you are home," started Petunia, "we can discuss this camp idea the girls are interested in."

"Oh, so that's what all this is about."

"We made a list Daddy about why you and mommy don't have to worry," said Sasha quite proudly.

"You did? Well I would be very interested in seeing this list."

Sasha and Brady Boe ran quickly to the bedroom to retrieve the list. Brady Boe whispered to Sasha before going back into the kitchen. "We must remain calm Sasha, or else they will think we can't handle ourselves at camp."

"Okay, Brady Boe. I'll be calm."

No sooner than Sasha was back in the kitchen, she excitedly gave Mike the list. "Look, Daddy. Read it now!"

Brady Boe just rolled her eyes. She should have known that Sasha did not have a calm bone in her body. Petunia raised her hand to get everyone's attention. "I did call Camp Firefly today to get some information. I also called Taylor's mom to see what her experience has been with them."

Brady Boe looked surprised. She did not know her mom had called anyone. She wished she could have been a fly on the wall to hear what Taylor's mom said. She kept her fingers crossed behind her back. If their parents allowed them to go to camp, they would have so much fun. It would be like a reunion of friends.

Mike and Petunia sat down at the kitchen table to read the list that Brady Boe and Sasha made earlier that day. Every now and then, they would look at each other and grin. Brady Boe and Sasha stood nearby watching every move. At one point, Mike burst out in a bellowing laughter. Brady Boe could hardly stand it. They were having too much fun with their list. It must have got to Sasha too because she could resist no longer.

"What is so funny? We didn't mean to make you guys laugh?" she cried.

After calming themselves down for a moment, Mike spoke. "This is actually pretty good."

"You two made some very good points about how you would stay safe." Added Petunia.

"Why were you guys laughing?" asked Sasha again.

"Well, we were trying to imagine in the event of someone attacking you, Sasha would scream in her Hyena voice and Brady Boe would unleash her Judo. On a more serious note, you two have never stayed anywhere for a week without us. It makes me a little nervous."

"There will be adults around, and I will not let Brady Boe out of my sight—only when she has to go to the bathroom and only for number two though." Sasha started to say more but Brady Boe thought she went far enough.

"I think what Sasha is trying to say is that we understand your concern, and we are going to be responsible and look out for each other."

"Very well put, Brady Boe. I think my little girl is growing up," said Mike.

"Yes, you sound confident. I like that," co-signed Petunia.

On the inside, Brady Boe felt good. She did something that even surprised her. She spoke to grown-ups with confidence, and she meant every word. She wanted to say more, but all this was too emotional for her already. She wanted to go to camp just as bad as Sasha did, but she also knew why her mom and dad were concerned. Her face felt warm. She wanted to run to her room. Sasha came up to her and put her arm around her. If Sasha said anything, Brady Boe thought she would lose it. Yet, Sasha did not say a word. She just stood there with her. Mike finally spoke again.

"Petunia, I think we should let them go."

Sasha immediately screamed and started jumping up and down.

Mike held up a hand. "Hold up Sasha, we need to hear what your mom has to say."

Sasha gathered herself once again, and stood quietly next to Brady Boe. The suspense was killing Brady Boe. She did not know how long she could stand there. The moments it took her mom to respond felt like years.

"Why not", said Petunia. "My only concern is for your safety and just hearing you two talk with confidence assures me that you will be aware of your surroundings. So, go have fun!"

Sasha threw her arms around each of her parent's neck, and then turned to Brady Boe. Brady Boe surprised her and opened her arms to receive a hug.

"Okay, Sasha. Don't suffocate me!"

Petunia and Mike laughed. Marcus joined in not wanting to miss any of the excitement.

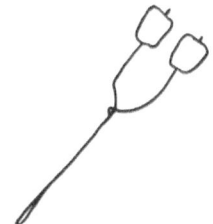

That night Brady Boe could hardly get to sleep. She could hardly wait until the next day to call her friends and let them know. She decided to write in her journal to calm her nerves.

Dear Journal,

Today marks a first in the history of my life. I think Iona would have been proud of me. I spoke up and made sense. Mrs. Ramsey would be proud too. I am so excited. We are going camping, and it is going to be so much fun! I can't wait to tell Terra, Margie, and Taylor. I must go to sleep now. There will be plenty of planning to do.

Chapter 2
Help for Margie

The first one up, Brady Boe showered and dressed as quick as she could. She wanted to get started on her day. Still excited over getting to go to camp, Brady Boe wanted to visit Taylor first thing to let her know.

"Sasha, wake up." Brady Boe stood near Sasha's bed ready to shake her if she did not respond right away.

"What time is it, Brady Boe?" grumbled Sasha.

"It's early. I need you to get up and get dressed pronto, Sasha. We need to go to Taylor's right after breakfast."

"Really, why so early?"

Brady Boe could not believe Sasha of all people was giving her a hard time about this. She was the excitable one. "Did you forget about camping, Sasha?"

It was like night and day. Sasha popped up, and jumped out of bed. "Is that today Brady Boe? Oh my, I have to get ready fast!" Sasha did a little dance before running into her closet to grab her small suitcase.

"No, silly. We are not going camping today. I just want to go tell Taylor our good news. Then, I have to call Margie and Terra."

Sasha looked disappointed for a minute. Then, she quickly recovered and humored Brady Boe by getting ready as quickly as possible. Both girls raced through eating cereal and toast before yelling to their parents that they would be running to tell Taylor the good news.

As soon as Brady Boe reached her hand up to knock on Taylor's door, Taylor swung the door open. "Good morning," said Taylor loudly. It took them by surprise. "It's okay, guys. I saw you coming from across the street, and I knew you must have some exciting news to tell me!"

"Actually we do," said Sasha. Brady Boe quickly covered Sasha's mouth. "We will tell her together Sasha. On the count of three." Brady Boe counted, "One… two… three!" Brady Boe and Sasha burst out at the same time, "We are going to camp!" Soon, all three girls were jumping up and down screaming in excitement. All the noise caused Taylors parents to ask what was going on. After Taylor explained, the parents continued on their way to fetch morning coffee.

"I'm so glad you guys are going. We are going to have so much fun." The girls sat on Taylor's front steps and talked for a while about all the fun things they were going to do at camp. The morning sun started feeling too hot. Brady Boe suggested they call Terra and Margie to see if they were going.

Back at home, Mike, Petunia, and Marcus were awake. They were eating breakfast in the kitchen. Brady Boe asked to call Terra and Margie. When she got the go ahead, she became nervous. She contemplated having Sasha start the call. She would get on the call after a moment. It was ridiculous she could admit, but it also felt awkward to say hi and ask to speak to her friend. She felt that she did not have a phone voice. Sasha did not care about all that. She just seemed to engage life, whether phone calls or otherwise, without thinking. Brady Boe finally decided to divide the task. Taylor would dial the numbers, and Sasha would ask for them. Once they were on the line, Brady Boe would talk to them. A team approach makes sense, she thought.

Things went smoothly. Terra was extremely excited that Brady Boe would be going to camp. She made that evident by screaming into the phone as if she had won the Publisher's Clearing House sweepstakes. Terra wanted them to call her right back after they talked with Margie. They promised, and took their positions to carry out the next call. Sasha seemed to talk with ease to the adults that came on the line first. Brady Boe was glad Sasha was so willing to appease her. She would never get through that part. Unfortunately, Margie did not have good news. Her parents could not afford to send her to camp. Brady Boe knew it would not be the same without Margie. She knew Margie really wanted to go. She could feel the disappointment in her voice. Margie told Brady Boe that they should have a good time without her. Maybe she would be able to attend next summer. Brady Boe's mind was racing. She had to think of something fast. She wanted her friend to go to camp. It hit her. Sasha and Taylor knew immediately that she had an idea. Brady Boe told Margie she would call her back. She told her to ask her parents if she could come over today. Margie said a quiet ok and hung up.

Taylor could not wait to hear what Brady Boe had come up with. "Alright, let's hear it," she said eagerly. Sasha leaned in closer, ears perked for what Brady Boe was going to say.

"Well, you guys know Margie can't go because her parents don't have the money."

They both nodded. Brady Boe was unaware that Petunia had come and was standing behind her.

"I think we should come up with some Ideas to raise enough money to help her go to camp. I really want her to go, and money is the only thing in her way. My first idea is a Lemonade stand. I want to have Terra and Margie over to brainstorm more ideas with us."

"Spoken like a true captain," applauded Petunia.

"Mom," said Brady Boe surprised to turn and see Petunia standing behind her. Her face flushed. She was slightly embarrassed.

"What you said, Honey, was great, and I will make the Lemonade," offered Petunia.

Sasha got excited. "We are going to have so much fun! I'll design the signs for the sale."

"You do make the best lemonade, Mrs. Wells," added Taylor.

"Why thank you, Taylor. I'll have some more to taste by the time you have your brainstorming meeting later."

Cheers went up.

"Thanks, Mommy," said Brady Boe feeling less embarrassed about taking charge.

"Your welcome, Honey. Now, go ahead and call your friends back. Your dad can help you build the lemonade stand when you're ready."

The girls called Terra and Margie back. They both confirmed they would be arriving in the next hour. This gave Brady Boe, Sasha, and Taylor time to see what supplies they had on hand for the lemonade sale. Marcus somehow attached himself to Sasha's side. Wherever she went, he went. Sasha could be quite nurturing with him. Besides, he did not want to miss any of the excitement.

When Terra and Margie arrived, a buzz of excitement ensued about five minutes. No clear words were spoken, just laughter, and a lot of screaming. Once things settled a bit, Brady Boe introduced Terra and Margie to her parents. Sasha hugged them both of course, and led them to the back patio to begin the meeting. Brady Boe realized she forgot to introduce Terra and Margie to Taylor. She felt bad for a moment until she looked over and saw Taylor talking with them as if she knew them already. Taylor and Sasha were just alike, she thought. They never seemed to be scared of making new friends.

Brady Boe took a deep breath and got everyone's attention. "I called this meeting so we could find a way to help Margie raise money to go to camp." Margie looked surprised and touched. Brady Boe decided not to look at her because she needed to focus. Sasha reached over and lovingly touched Margie on the hand.

"I came up with one idea: to have a lemonade stand. We may need another idea to make sure we make enough money. Any ideas?"

"I got one," yelled Taylor raising her hand. Not waiting for permission Taylor blurted out, "How about a dog walking service?"

Terra nodded. "I like it!"

"What do you think Margie," asked Brady Boe.

"All I can say is falemnderit." Margie struggled to hold her tears back but she lost the battle. One rolled down her rosy cheek.

In a flash Sasha was at Margie's side holding her hand and whispering, "It's okay."

"What did you say," asked Terra? It sounded like you offered us food. This apparently was funny to Taylor whose laugh triggered Brady Boe to laugh. Then, Sasha laughed too. Soon, Margie could not help it. She joined in too.

"No silly. I said thank you in Albanian. I've never had friends that care about me like you guys do. I will help as much as I can."

Brady Boe could see a dramatic presentation welling up in Sasha as Margie was talking. If she did not stop her, they would never get anything done.

Sasha stood up. "Aww don't worry Margie, we are going to make sure you have enough money to go to camp. I just want to take this moment..."

"Stop right there, Sasha. We must continue with our meeting. We have lots to do." Sasha looked disappointed, but she sat down promising to share her speech later. "We need someone to make signs for the lemonade sale and the dog walking service. We are going to post these signs all over the neighborhood. Make them colorful and flashy.

"I can do that!" yelled Sasha.

"I'll help her!" yelled Taylor.

"Great! The rest of us will help dad build and paint the Lemonade stand," said Brady Boe. Everyone scattered to get busy. Marcus refused to be left out. He was still right at Sasha's heels. She kept him busy helping to color the signs. Mike was already in the garage hammering away when Brady Boe, Terra and Margie came out. It was a hot day, and sweat was running down his face.

"Wow, Dad. You almost have it done. It looks great!"

Mike looked up surprised that he had an audience. "Hi, girls."

Brady Boe introduced Terra and Margie. "Nice to meet you girls. You guys must be here to help me finish putting this stand together?"

"Yes, we are, Mr. Wells," answered Margie eagerly.

Mike handed Margie the hammer and a nail. The girls took turns hammering, but did not make much progress. They decided to look for paint in order to paint the stand when Mike was done. At noon, Petunia stopped everyone from working to serve lunch. She did not get any arguments. Their work was just about done, and they were hungry and thirsty. Brady Boe was content, not just for the delicious turkey sandwiches and cold lemonade her mom filled them with. She felt like she was making a difference. It was a little overwhelming to think about, so she tucked it away for later when she was by herself. She certainly did not want Sasha to see her feeling emotional.

After lunch, everyone stood outside and viewed the lemonade stand. It had quite the look. It was painted pink with yellow borders. The word "Lemonade" dried in blue paint, Terra's favorite color. Margie added her signature flower design in each corner. Mike and Petunia gave the girls a thumb's up.

"We have one last thing to do guys. That is, after mom takes a few pictures of us in front of the famous Lemonade stand."

"What's that, Brady Boe?" asked Taylor.

"We have go post up these posters and hand out these flyers. The events start the day after tomorrow. Is that alright, Mom?"

"If that's the case. Then, I had better get started making a few batches of lemonade. I will give you girls one hour to hang up your posters and distribute your flyers in the neighbor."

Brady Boe noticed Petunia's worried expression. "Don't worry, Mom. We will be careful and stay together."

Petunia smiled at her and followed Mike and Marcus into the house.

Sasha was quite proud of the posters they made. She loved making designs, and she made sure to put her signature touch on each one of them. Taylor and Marcus gave her plenty of ideas and made a few themselves. As the girls headed down the street, they discussed how they would go about the dog walking service. They made an agreement not to walk big dogs being that Margie was scared of the big ones.

There were a few people out walking. Sasha did not hesitate to offer them a flyer. Brady Boe was glad to have her there. She knew Sasha would do well at making everyone they came across aware of their moneymaking efforts. Brady Boe grew a little nervous as they were about to walk past Iona's house. Taylor saw her slow down.

"Is everything alright, Brady Boe?"

"Oh! No. I was just thinking about something." Brady Boe tried not to draw any attention to what she saw, but it was too late. Sasha saw the black car too. She caught Brady Boe's hand and rushed her past Iona's house. Margie looked concerned, but did not say anything. She stayed close to Brady Boe the rest of the way.

The girls made sure they put a flyer or poster at every corner in the neighborhood. They even walked up to a few doors of the people that looked like they were at home. Sasha and Taylor did all the talking of course. Terra teased her about being shy. Brady Boe decided she would give the last flyer out to the house nestled in the cul-de-sac. She knew an older woman lived there with two dogs. She had never met the woman, but she had to prove to Terra that she could do it.

"You guys have to come up to the house with me, but I'll do all the talking."

"Don't worry Brady Boe, we will be right there with you," said Terra in a joking tone.

Brady Boe led the way up the stony path and up the creaky stairs. She rang the doorbell once. Nothing happened. She rang it again. That is when she heard a voice from the other side of the door. It did not sound at all friendly. Brady Boe braced herself. She was not going to let the situation get the best of her. After all, she had to prove to Terra in particular that she could do this. The door opened with a squeak.

"Why are you ringing my doorbell like that?" grumbled the elderly woman who appeared behind the screen door.

"I...I..I...wanted to...to.. give you this," stuttered Brady Boe holding up the two flyers.

Soon two small dogs were barking like crazy around the door. The woman yelled at them to be quiet. They immediately stopped and resorted to doing their best to sniff through the screen door. Brady Boe could tell Sasha was ready to jump in at any moment. Terra and Margie looked a little scared by the elderly woman. Margie grabbed Terra's hand.

"Well, what is it child!? Does it look like I have all day to stand here?"

Brady Boe thought she must be the meanest woman in the world. She calmly spoke, though her voice was a little shaky. "We are trying to raise money for camp for our friend. We would like for you to buy some lemonade and use our dog walking service."

Sasha moved in closer as if to get a better look at the woman. "Do you have a name?" she asked.

Brady Boe gave her the look intended to communicate that she should stop immediately, but Sasha ignored her.

The woman tried to straighten up her hunched over back to respond to Sasha's question. "I am the late Mrs. Windleton, if you must know."

"My name is Sasha and this is Brady Boe, Terra, Margie and Taylor. I didn't think old people were mean. Our last old friend was really nice."

Brady Boe could feel all the blood rush to her face. She never expected Sasha to say what she did.

"My grandma is kind of mean sometimes." Taylor then chimed in. "For some reason she just doesn't like a lot of noise."

The woman seemed disarmed, not knowing what to say at that moment. She hurriedly opened the door a fraction and took the flyers. "Now go play. I got things to do," she snapped.

The girls needed no further warning. They ran down the same stony path they came up. Once they were all at a safe distance away from the house, Terra patted Brady Boe on the back.

"Well done, Chap."

"Of course she had to be the meanest lady in the neighborhood," Brady Boe pointed out.

"I'm pooped. I think we should be getting home," said Margie using Sasha's shoulder to lean on.

Margie's and Terra's mom were waiting at the house when they arrived. Everyone said their good-byes and parted in different directions. Taylor promised she would see them the next day.

After dinner, Brady Boe was exhausted she grabbed her journal and climbed into her bed. Out her bedroom window, the color changed to dusk. Evening had set in. So much had happened that day. She did not know where to begin.

Dear Journal,

I'd like to think of today as the day I felt like a leader. I have to admit I was a little scared that something wouldn't work out right. But, so far so good. We are going to make lots of money, and Margie will be able to go to camp. It was fun having everyone over working together. I really miss Ms. Iona; she would have been here too. I know she would have baked something for us. That's just how she was. I don't know about Mrs. Windleton, she was so rude in how she talked to us! Ms. Iona would have never done that. I wonder what makes her treat people that way. It can't just be that she's old. I'm glad Sasha said what she did to her. I saw the black car today parked at Ms. Iona's. Of course, I didn't get a glimpse of who might be driving it. I must get some sleep now. My eyes are about to close. Good night!

BB

Chapter 3
A Mysterious Note

Pure excitement woke Brady Boe and Sasha up early in the morning. The weather appeared to be on their side. The temperature was seventy-five degrees at six in the morning. The weather report spoke of a rise to record-breaking one hundred and five degrees by afternoon. For such an occasion, Brady Boe decided to wear her favorite purple baseball cap with her most beloved purple converse.

Sasha came dashing into her room. "Wow, don't you look cute, but look at me." Sasha twirled around Brady Boe's room allowing the wind she created to lift her pink poofy skirt.

"Isn't this the most perfect look for the grand opening of our lemonade sale?"

"I do believe it is, Sasha, especially if it's going to help us sell a lot of lemonade today."

"I just had a great idea, Brady Boe. You could wear my purple skirt, the one like this," Sasha said this while pointing to her skirt. "We could be twins!"

Brady Boe cringed. "No way, Sasha! I love you, but I am not wearing that twirly, girlie, tutu of a skirt to sell lemonade. Let's get our roles straight."

Sasha looked somewhat confused.

"I'm the money master mind, and you are the movie star!"

Sasha liked the title of movie star. "Thanks, Brady Boe. I must now go and practice signing my autograph."

Brady Boe just shook her head. She knew it did not take much to get her sister going.

The fragrance of fresh squeezed lemons over took the entire house. Several buckets filled with halved gutted lemons sat around the back patio and kitchen. In the fridge, Brady Boe found three huge five-gallon containers and a few gallon pitchers filled with Petunia's sweet lemonade. Petunia was finishing a couple more gallons on the back patio when she heard Brady Boe stirring around in the kitchen.

"Good morning, Brady Boe," she called.

Brady Boe followed her mother's voice to the back patio. "Mom, you must have been up all night to make all that lemonade."

"Let's just say when your dad retired to bed at 2 am, it was me and marathon of episodes from I Love Lucy to Gilligan's Island." Her mom's eyes looked tired, but Brady Boe could see the contentment in them. "I think you guys should have enough for your sale today. The cups are on the table."

Sasha entered the room and made her presence known by bursting out in song. She stopped abruptly to comment on all the buckets of squeezed lemons. "Somebody has been busy!"

"That somebody is now going to take a nap and let two energetic girls clean these buckets up." Petunia kissed both her girls on their foreheads as she passed through on her way to find her bed.

Sasha assessed the mess. "Shall we start?"

"Yes," said Brady Boe in a hurry. "The sooner we get this cleaned up the sooner we can set up the lemonade stand before Margie and Terra get here."

"Yeah, good thinking, Brady Boe."

It was nine o'clock when Mike helped the girls pull the lemonade stand out of the garage. Taylor had already joined them. She was equally excited about the sale. She told them that her mom and dad would be by in a bit to be their first customers.

"Did we ever decide on a price," asked Taylor.

"I say seventy-five cents. Because most stands sell it for twenty-five cents, and we are doing it for a special cause," said Brady Boe.

"Why not one dollar?" added Sasha. "After all the lemonade is homemade."

"You have a point, Sasha," Brady Boe replied.

"Do you think people will still buy it if it's a dollar? That might be too much," commented Taylor.

"You have a point too Taylor. We don't want to break their pocket book, as they say." Brady Boe did not know which way to go.

"Come on girls, we have hot sticky weather on our side. These people will do anything to get a cold drink, and we will have it for them. Besides that, lemons are good for you!"

"You make a good argument, Sasha, but should we wait and let Margie and Terra help decide?" asked Brady Boe.

"No, Brady Boe. We should decide now. I agree with Sasha. It is going to be sweltering today as my mom would say. They may even want two cups," offered Taylor.

Brady Boe hit her imaginary judge gavel down. "The decision has been made. One dollar for each cup of homemade lemonade!"

Taylor and Sasha nodded in agreement.

Mike called Brady Boe inside to get the phone. She almost felt anxious, but then realized it had to be Margie or Terra. Otherwise, she was not ready to risk sounding awkward randomly speaking to a stranger on the other end. It was Margie letting her know she would be there soon. Terra was picking her up. After hanging up the phone Brady Boe jumped on her bike, and left Taylor and Sasha to finish setting things up. She wanted to do a quick ride through the neighborhood to make sure their signs by the main roads were still in place. Brady Boe was going so fast and not really paying attention. She did not see the U-Haul truck parked outside of Iona's house until she was right in front of it. Two men were coming out of her house carrying her furniture to the truck. The mysterious black car sat parked right behind the truck. Brady Boe wondered if this car was the same black car that chased her and Sasha on their way home from school. She never looked at the car long enough to get a good look at it. There were tons of black cars in the world. She decided to hurry past anyways, not wanting any trouble. For a moment, she felt sad for Iona. She still wanted to go to her house and listen to her stories. Iona would be so happy about what they were doing today. Brady Boe wondered if her birth mom was anything like Iona. If she was, she probably would have showed up at the meeting they set up. Iona would have never stood me up, Brady Boe thought. Brady Boe forced herself to stop thinking about all of it for the moment. It was just too confusing. How could her birth mom not rush to be with her? Yet, Brady Boe was not angry enough to forget her.

Shortly after Brady Boe made it back home, Margie and Terra arrived. Taylor and Sasha filled them in on how they came up with the price of the lemonade. Margie was just grateful for the help. Terra was ready for the fun. Marcus made his way outside, not wanting to be excluded from any of the action. Sasha found a chair that was just his size and sat him behind the lemonade stand.

"You are going to be our little helper today, okay?"

Marcus gave Sasha a soldier's salute and a big grin, letting her know he was pleased with his job.

The temperature was climbing already, though it was still morning. Mike placed one gallon of lemonade in a cooler full of ice behind the stand. The girls entertained themselves with talk about camp while waiting for thirsty customers. It was not long before a big black car crept up slowly and stopped on the side close to the curb. Brady Boe and Sasha froze immediately.

"Do you guys know this person?" Their sudden action compelled Terra to ask.

Mike had already gone back inside the house. Sasha shot Brady Boe a nervous look. Margie volunteered to pour the first cup of lemonade for their very first customer. The door to the black car slowly opened. Sasha was already half-way to the house to get Mike just in case of trouble. The little old gray haired Mrs. Windleton finally made her face seen.

Brady Boe let herself breathe normal again. Sasha ran back to the stand. Terra just stood with a question still on her face.

"Well, I hope this lemonade is good. The only reason I came by is because I had to get my medication from the pharmacy. It is entirely too hot out here!" Mrs. Windleton was holding the flyer the girls had given her yesterday as she walked carefully and slowly to the stand. The girls did not know if she was talking to them or just muttering to herself, but no one dared ask. They just waited. Marcus stared at Mrs. Windleton as she reached for the surface of the stand for support to lean on. Her bony, wrinkled hand made him curious, and he reached out to touch it with his finger.

"Aren't you a cute as a button? Don't get old my little boy."

"Marcus has a long way to go before that happens," replied Sasha.

"Oh, I remember you. You're the sassy one. Give me my cup of lemonade already. I'm thirsty," urged Mrs. Windleton.

Margie handed her the cup she poured. When she finished drinking Mrs. Windleton laid a dollar bill on the table, and turned to leave. Before getting in her car she turned around, "Who is Brady Boe?"

Brady Boe raised her hand.

"Come here child, and get this flyer. I want my Tiny walked tomorrow. My number is on the back of this flyer."

Brady Boe walked over to Mrs. Windleton, and took the flyer. "Thank you, Mrs. Windleton, for buying a cup of lemonade."

"Well, whatever. Whoever made it did a good job. I must get out of this heat now."

She is certainly no Ms. Iona, thought Brady Boe watching her leave. When Mrs. Windleton was out of sight, the girls celebrated their first dollar by taking turns fanning it around before placing it in a recipe box they had selected earlier from the kitchen.

Business picked up quite a bit after Mrs. Windleton left. The cars would almost pass by until they looked over and saw the lemonade sign. People that were out walking in the neighborhood stopped to say hi and get a refreshing drink. Petunia received many compliments on her lemonade. The girls smiled and kindly said thank you to each one.

The lemonade pitchers in the cooler were getting low, so Brady Boe, Sasha, and Taylor ran inside for more. Margie and Terra filled three cups and set them aside. They got caught up talking about camp until Ryan from school came riding up on his bike. Marcus took that moment to get him a drink. He took one of the three cups and drunk the lemonade down. He then threw the cup in the garbage under the stand and sat back on his stool. The girls never paid him any attention.

"Hi, Terra. Hi, Margie," said Ryan.

Margie looked surprised and nudged Terra. Through clenched teeth, she asked Terra, "What is he doing here?"

Terra had a goofy smile and replied, "I invited him."

Ryan got off his bike and laid it in the grass. There was a moment of awkwardness while Ryan made his way over to the lemonade stand. Margie watched her friend Terra. She did not know what was going on, but something was different about Ryan and Terra.

Brady Boe, Sasha, and Taylor finally came back with three more jugs of lemonade. Brady Boe nearly stopped in her tracks when she saw Ryan. Her first thought was that he was there to make trouble. Trouble was his middle name at school. Terra must have noticed the expression on her face and commented on Ryan's behalf.

"It's okay, Brady Boe. He's just here to buy some lemonade."

"Hi, Brady Boe," said Ryan sheepishly.

"Hi, Ryan, she answered suspiciously.

"Is it okay if I buy a cup of Lemonade?" he asked.

Brady Boe didn't know what Ryan was up to, but if he wanted to buy a cup of lemonade for a dollar then she was going to let him.

"Sure, you can buy a cup."

Terra ran over everyone trying to get one of the cups they had poured already for Ryan.

"Wait a minute. We had three cups here."

Margie looked over. "We sure did. I poured them myself."

"I think somebody got thirsty," Sasha said pointing to Marcus's lemonade mustache.

"You little sneaky boy," said Margie reaching over to pinch his cheeks. "How did you do that without us seeing you?"

Marcus jumped down off the stool and ran in the house laughing. That cracked Sasha up.

Meanwhile Brady Boe was paying attention to something else. She noticed Terra being pretty friendly with Ryan. She made a mental note to talk to her later about him.

More customers came in spurts throughout the day. The recipe box was getting full of money. At about 5 o'clock the girls were down to their last jug. Taylor's mom and dad made their way over to get a cup while picking Taylor up. They commented on what a good thing the girls were doing to help their friend. Sasha ran to give Taylor a hug and told her she would see her tomorrow. Terra's mom came shortly after that. Terra told Brady Boe she would call her in the morning to let her know if she would be able to go dog walking with them. Brady Boe did not want her to leave yet. She had some explaining to do about Ryan.

Sasha and Brady Boe decided to start cleaning things up while Margie stayed at the stand just in case any last minute customers stopped by. Just as Brady Boe and Sasha went into the house, a fancy black car pulled along the curb rather fast in Margie's estimation. She thought it was Mrs. Windleton back for more lemonade. Margie had a cup ready for her. Instead, a woman who was not Mrs. Windleton jumped out of the car. In what seemed like one motion, she threw an envelope on the stand, jumped back into her car, and sped off. Margie's mouth was still fixed to say her rehearsed line offering a cool cup of lemonade when the woman sped off. Things happened so fast Margie could hardly describe what the woman looked like.

Brady Boe and Sasha brought their dad back with them to help move the lemonade stand back into the garage.

"Margie, what happened? You look like we have been robbed," said Brady Boe not sure how to read the expression on Margie's face. In Brady Boe's mind that would be the worst thing that could happen to them right now.

Margie handed Brady Boe the envelope the woman left on the stand. "Here. This woman in a black car just left this for you. She did not even buy any lemonade. She took off so fast that I didn't get her name. The envelope has your name on it, Brady Boe. Maybe she is a relative."

Margie's words stopped Mike from taking down the stand. He looked at Brady Boe holding the envelope and letter in her hands.

Brady Boe had already read the words. A crisp one dollar bill fell to the ground.

"Let me see the letter, Brady Boe," said Mike.

Sasha walked over to Margie. "Margie, think hard now. Do you remember anything about this person?"

"No, Sasha. It happened so fast. She zoomed up right in front of the stand, jumped out, and threw the envelope on the stand. Oh, I do remember one thing. She had on sunglasses and a big hat. I couldn't make out anything about her face though. She never said anything."

Mike read the letter.

Brady Boe could see the words from the letter flashing through her head.

It wasn't my fault!
They want to keep you from me.
Your B.M.

Margie could feel the tension in the air. "Did I do something wrong?"

"It's okay, Margie. You did nothing wrong. Someone just left a note for Brady Boe, and we don't know who it could be," said Mike hoping make the air lighter.

"Well, she did leave a dollar. That was nice of her," added Margie.

Sasha wanted to ask Brady Boe what the letter said but decided it probably was not the best time judging how her dad and sister looked.

"Why don't you girls go inside and count the money you made today. I will finish clearing things up out here," offered Mike. He placed the letter in his back pocket.

Margie took the recipe box and followed Sasha into the house. Brady Boe glanced back at her dad wondering what he was going to do with the letter. Surely, he would show Petunia. All she knew is she did not want anything to stop her from going to camp.

The girls settled on the back deck to count the money. After pouring themselves a cup of lemonade, they divided the money up. Each counted their portion. Then, they added it all together.

Sasha made the announcement. "We have a total of seventy-five dollars!"

"Oh no!" said Margie, "We don't have enough. We still need fifty dollars."

"Don't give up too fast, Margie. We still have the dog walking service tomorrow," said Brady Boe.

"That's right, Brady Boe. Mrs. Windleton already hired us. What fun that will be," said Sasha rather sarcastically.

"You gals are great! We did really well today. I really don't mean to sound ungrateful."

"Don't worry Margie. We are getting you to camp," promised Brady Boe.

Petunia poked her head out the door to inform Margie that her mom was there to pick her up. Margie thanked everyone and promised to see them the next day.

That night Sasha stood in Brady Boe's bedroom door. "So, what did the letter say?"

Brady Boe hesitated, wondering if she should tell Sasha.

"Come on Brady Boe I want to know."

"Alright, it said, "It wasn't my fault." Brady Boe purposely held back what else was on the letter. She didn't want Sasha getting all excited.

"Do you think it was from your birth mom?"

"Could be," answered Brady Boe nonchalantly.

"I don't like her getting that close, Brady Boe. Do you think she is going to try and take you away?"

"Don't worry about it, Sasha. She wouldn't do that."

"How do you know that?"

"I just do, Sasha. Now, get some sleep. We have to spend time with the mean Mrs. Windleton tomorrow.

Sasha yawned and slowly turned to do what her sister instructed.

Brady Boe wrote in her journal that night.

Dear Journal,

Today went great! I feel disturbed about a couple things though. First, there is something going on with Terra and Ryan. At school, she couldn't stand him. Today, she actually ran over us to get his lemonade. I will have to get the full story out of her. The second thing is the mysterious note that was left for me at the lemonade stand. I can't help but wonder what if I had been outside when she came. What would've happened then? If it was my birth mom, I want to believe that it wasn't her fault, but I don't really know what to think. I know dad will tell mommy about it, and she will worry. I just want to go to camp.

Good night!

Chapter 4
Mrs. Ramsey's Wisdom

"Today, pancakes and sausage are in order because we have lots of walking to do."

Brady Boe peered at Sasha through half open eyes. Sasha was standing over her bed talking rather loud. "Sasha, I'm not even awake yet!"

"Well, wake up. Mom has fresh hot pancakes ready. Besides, Mrs. Windleton already called and said she needed us to come at 9 o'clock sharp.

"Great," growled Brady Boe.

"I took the liberty of calling Taylor. She'll be over in just a bit to eat pancakes with us. I thought you would like to call Terra and Margie."

"Wow, Sasha. You are on it this morning."

Sasha struck a proud pose before going back to the kitchen.

Brady Boe turned to glance at the clock. It read 8 o'clock. That meant she had to hurry with her shower, eat breakfast, and get to Mrs. Windleton's in one hour.

After her shower and getting dressed as fast as she could, Brady Boe felt eager to get started. Sasha was on the phone with another customer when Brady Boe walked into the kitchen. Taylor was already sitting at the table, her mouth stuffed with pancakes. She waved at Brady Boe.

"Boe eat pannie cakes," greeted Marcus. She rubbed his head and took the plate Petunia handed her with two fluffy, buttered pancakes and two peaceful slices of turkey bacon. Brady Boe was in heaven for a moment as she devoured the bacon first.

Sasha hung up the phone. "We have another customer, girls. This lady wants us to walk her three dogs. Two of them are Labradors, and the other is a German Shepard."

"Those are big dogs," said Mike.

"We can handle it dad. Speedy was big too," replied Sasha.

"You're right about that. He was good size," agreed Mike.

The mention of Speedy made Brady Boe miss him again. He was such a good dog, she thought. Brady Boe focused her attention to the last few bites of pancakes. When she was done, Sasha and Taylor huddled around her while she called Terra and Margie.

Brady Boe hung up the phone after talking with Margie.

"Well?" prompted Sasha.

Brady Boe sighed. "She has to stay home and watch her little brother for a while. Then, maybe when her parents get home from work, she could come over. But, it's a big maybe. I think they depend on her a lot for things because they work so much."

"She could bring her little brother with us," suggested Taylor. "How old is he?"

Brady Boe thought for a moment. "I think he is around four years old or close to it. But it's okay. When we get this money for her to go to camp, she will get a break."

"That's right, Brady Boe. Call Terra now. It's getting close to 9 o'clock," urged Sasha. "Money is ready to be made, and dogs are waiting to be walked."

Brady Boe picked up the phone and called Terra. After a couple okay's she hung up.

"That was quick," said Taylor.

"Yeah, looks like it's going to be just us for now."

"Well, let's take a minute before we go to plan out our route," suggested Sasha.

"Good idea, Sasha." Taylor volunteered to write down the addresses.

Sasha recited the list from her memory, "First is Mrs. Windleton. She only has one dog, and our first five dollars. Next, we have the lady with the three dogs. That's gives us fifteen dollars."

Brady Boe raised her hand. Sasha paused.

"If we are out walking the dogs, how are we going to get calls for more customers?"

Petunia had been busy washing the breakfast dishes and clearing the table while the girls planned. "Can I help you girls?"

"You want to walk dogs with us, Mommy?" Asked Sasha.

"No, honey. But, I could take messages if someone should call. When you girls are finished with your second customer, check in with me. Maybe even grab a bite to eat."

"That sounds like a plan," said Brady Boe. "Let's go!"

With ten minutes to spare, the girls pleaded with Mike to drop them off at Mrs. Windleton's house on his way to work. Mike gave in, and they all headed out in a rush.

Petunia watched after them for a moment. After Mike showed her the note left for Brady Boe, she felt a little uneasy letting them walk around the neighborhood. She wondered if Lily really was trying to get Brady Boe back. None of this started until after Iona died. She wondered if Iona said something to Lily.

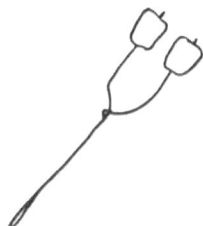

Mrs. Windleton was sitting on her front porch when Mike pulled into her driveway. He waved at her. He then turned to the girls and told them to be safe and remember to check in with Petunia. They assured him they would and got out of the car.

Mrs. Windleton had a cross look on her face. Tiny barked as they approached the porch. Taylor shot Brady Boe a look, which Brady Boe interpreted as, "Is this really worth doing?" Brady Boe thought the same, but it was to help Margie go to camp. That is how she settled it in her mind. She convinced herself that it was not going to be forever. Sasha on the other hand, seemed cool as a cucumber. When they finally made it to the top of the stairs, Mrs. Windleton let them have it.

Mrs. Windleton looked cross at them over the top rim of her glasses. "Did you ladies forget your duty this morning? Tiny here has been ready since 8 o'clock this morning. He is now restless and unfocused."

Neither Brady Boe nor Taylor could not open their mouth to respond, they looked puzzled.

Sasha continued to walk towards Tiny and placed her hand out for him to sniff it. Then she looked up at Mrs. Windleton, "It is now 9 o'clock, the time set on the phone. There is no need to be cross with us. Tiny seems to be just fine."

Tiny licked Sasha's hand and tried to lean on her when she rubbed his head. Meanwhile Brady Boe and Taylor swallowed hard, not knowing how Mrs. Windleton would take Sasha's words.

"I beg your pardon child," replied Mrs. Windleton. "My Tiny needs time to get adjusted to new people before I just send him off."

Brady Boe could see Sasha ready to respond. She grabbed her arm and under her breath she said, "Sasha, no", as stern as she could.

Taylor just watched wide-eyed and glad Sasha had the guts to say anything because she sure did not. Sasha ignored Brady Boe's quiet, stern protest.

"With all due respect Mrs. Windleton, Tiny is not the one who needs time to get to know us. He likes us just fine. You are the one who needs to get adjusted. If you want a friend, treating us this way is not how it is going to happen. We will kindly leave Tiny here and go about our way."

Mrs. Windleton's face turned beet red. "Your sassy mouth child is going to get you in a world of trouble. Is that how you feel too? She darted her beady, cold eyes at Brady Boe.

Brady boe could feel her hands trembling. She just hunched her shoulders and muttered a quiet, "I don't know."

"I figured as much," muttered Mrs. Windleton back. "I think you guys should be getting off on the walk. Tiny's nap time will be coming soon."

Sasha held her hand out.

Mrs. Windleton now looked confused.

"We need payment please," said Sasha.

"You haven't done the work yet!" argued Mrs. Windleton.

"We will take very good care of Tiny, but I don't trust you."

"Are you trying to call me some kind of criminal child?" Mrs. Windleton dug in her apron pocket and pulled out a folded five-dollar bill. "Here. Take it. I have no reason to flim-flam my end of the deal."

The girls made their way away from Mrs. Windleton's house as quickly as they could attach the leash to Tiny's collar. Once they were out of sight, Brady Boe and Taylor looked at Sasha in disbelief. Brady Boe did not know where to start.

"Oh, Sasha! I can't believe you spoke to Mrs. Windleton like that. You could get in trouble you know."

"How? You think she'll tell mom and dad? Well, I don't care. She deserved it. She needs a friend, Brady Boe, but she's being mean instead of nice."

"How do you know this, Sasha?" asked Brady Boe.

"I just do. For one thing, she would not have let us walk Tiny. I think she's lonely. But I refuse to be treated like that by her. Ms. Iona would never do that to us or anybody!"

Brady Boe nudged Taylor. "What do you think?"

"I think Sasha was brave. I probably would have run home. She was pretty mean."

"I know she was mean, but how did you know what to say Sasha? Did you hear mom and dad say that before, or was it something from a movie you saw?"

"No, Brady Boe. It wasn't from mom and dad. But, it did give me an opportunity to use my acting voice. They talk like that in the shows, you know."

"So that's where you get all that drama," teased Taylor.

The talk about Mrs. Windleton kept the girls going for Tiny's whole walk. When they returned Tiny back to Mrs. Windleton, he gave Sasha one more lick on the cheek before she handed him over. Mrs. Windleton said a quiet thank you and then disappeared behind the door.

"I think she's sad now," said Taylor.

"Don't be fooled, Taylor. She's too mean for that."

After the girls finished their next appointment walking three dogs, they were worn out. Each of them had a dog, and the dogs were mostly under control.

Petunia stood in front of the house looking out for the girls. Up the street, she soon saw them headed her way. She chuckled at the way they held on to each other as if they might pass out. Petunia knew they would be ready for lunch, so she hurried back in to get tuna sandwiches and three glasses of lemonade ready.

From the moment the girls stepped into the house, they complained about the heat. They took turns sharing with Petunia elements of their dog walking experience—everything except the part where Sasha got sassy with Mrs. Windleton. Sasha anticipated that Brady Boe or Taylor might talk about it. She was ready to defend her reasoning.

"Well," said Petunia, "I do have some good news."

"What is it, Mom," urged Sasha.

"Another lady called, and she wants her poodle walked this afternoon about 1 o'clock. I took down her name and address and left it by the phone. It's not too far, near the school I think. So, that gives you guys' time to eat and rest a bit before you go back out.

The girls hi-fived each other excited to have another customer. With their remaining time, Sasha chose to entertain Marcus by pretending to be his horse. Brady Boe and Taylor talked strategy about what else they could do to help Margie get more money.

"Do you think we will have all the money in time for camp next week, Brady Boe?" Asked Taylor.

"I don't know, Taylor. We need thirty more dollars. If we don't make it today, or tomorrow..."

Taylor did not let Brady Boe finish. "Don't worry, Brady Boe. I have twenty dollars my Nana gave me for my birthday this year. Then, we just have to come up with ten more."

"I don't know about that Taylor. I don't want you giving up your Nana money. Maybe we'll get more calls for dog walking today."

Sasha charged into the room. "Time to go girls! Wait. Why the serious looks?"

"We were just talking about what if we didn't get enough money for Margie. I told Brady Boe that I would give her the twenty dollars my Nana gave me for my birthday."

"Oh, Taylor. That is generous of you, but what if your Nana finds out?"

"Okay, let's go," interrupted Brady Boe. She did not want Sasha to go into one of her acting moments. She picked up the address by the phone and pushed her friend and sister out the door.

It did not take the girls long to find the address. The house was close to the school just as Petunia said. Sasha drew the shortest stick, so she knocked on the door. Just before Sasha poised her hand to knock, the door flew open, and Ms. Wilson grabbed her very excited poodle to keep it from running past the girls and out into the street.

"Hi, girls. Great timing. As you can see, Curly is rather excited. I'm Ms. Wilson."

"My name is Sasha. This is Brady Boe, my sister, and our friend Taylor."

"Nice to meet you girls, and thank you so much for walking Curly. I would do it myself, but to be honest, I saw your sign and thought why not take a break today and let someone else do it. Curly loves people."

Curly was already jumping up and down to greet them. Sasha held him while Brady Boe attached the leash. Curly led the way without hesitation.

The girls followed Curly's lead. He headed in the direction of the school playground. "Ms. Wilson is sure nicer than Mrs. Windleton," Taylor spoke up.

"Really, Taylor? Mrs. Windleton is not even a little nice."

"She was probably a bully when she was in school," added Sasha, "and just never grew out of it."

"All I know is she is mean and I feel sorry for Tiny," Taylor replied.

"Well, I think you are spending your time feeling sorry for the wrong animal. Tiny is treated like a king. You should feel sorry for her husband or her kids." Brady Boe tried to mimic the way Mrs.

Windleton spoke about Tiny's naptime. That made Sasha and Taylor laugh until they doubled over.

"Brady Boe, I didn't know you had such acting skills," teased Sasha.

Brady Boe blushed. After walking Curly for one more block, they started back to Ms. Wilson's house. Curly seemed to know his time was almost up. He stalled at every lawn they passed for a few minutes. Ms. Wilson was coming out the door when they arrived. Curly wagged his tail excitedly when he saw her.

"Thanks, girls. Here is your payment." She handed Brady Boe a crisp five-dollar bill.

They each patted Curly on the head and walked toward home. Brady Boe looked up surprised after they turned the corner. She saw a familiar face standing in front of the house they were passing.

"Brady Boe, how good to see you!"

Brady Boe tried to think of something to say fast. Sasha of course responded right away and shook Brady Boe's arm.

"Brady Boe, isn't that your teacher?"

"Yes, Sasha," said Brady Boe through clenched teeth.

Mrs. Ramsey had made her way to the sidewalk where the girls were standing. Brady Boe managed to find her voice, which came out somewhat squeaky. "Hi."

"You are still that shy, pretty girl. What a surprise! Let's see you are Brady Boe's little sister, is that right?" Mrs. Ramsey directed her question towards Sasha.

"Yes, and this is our friend Taylor.

"Nice to meet you, Taylor."

Taylor said a quick hello.

Brady Boe really did like Mrs. Ramsey. She did not know why talking to her was so difficult. She had no problems talking to her friends. It must be something with adults. Mrs. Ramsey seemed to have understood and never made anything out of it. Sasha started sharing what they were doing to help Margie go to camp. Stating that Brady Boe came up with the idea. Brady Boe and Taylor would add something in every now then, but Sasha did most of the talking.

After hearing all they said, Mrs. Ramsey turned to Brady Boe. "I knew you were captain material. Do you have a journal to record all your great ideas?"

"I have a diary," answered Brady Boe wondering if that was what Mrs. Ramsey was referencing.

"Stay right here, girls. I'll be right back."

The girls looked at each other curiously as Mrs. Ramsey disappeared into her house. When she returned, she had three books in her hand.

"Here, I have one for each of you." Mrs. Ramsey gave each of them a hardcover book with lined blank sheets of paper in them. The front cover had a picture of a sunset in a beach setting.

"These are some journals I had laying around. I want you girls to write in them often. It would be a nice spot to record those great ideas you come up with. You can even write out your life plans. I write in mine all the time."

"Thank you, Mrs. Ramsey! This is so cool. I think I will use mine for pictures though. I love to draw," explained Sasha.

"What a great idea," replied Mrs. Ramsey. "I like the way you think, Sasha."

Mrs. Ramsey then turned and winked at Brady Boe. I know someone else will be recording something great in hers too. Right, Brady Boe?"

Brady Boe flashed her biggest smile. "Yes, I will, Mrs. Ramsey."

"Good! That is exactly what I wanted to hear. Now, you girls get going, and enjoy camp!"

Taylor and Sasha yelled bye as they took off running. "Last one home is a ..." hollered Taylor.

Brady Boe gave Mrs. Ramsey a quick hug before running to catch up with Sasha and Taylor.

When Brady Boe finally caught up with Sasha and Taylor she leaned on them for support. The afternoon heat took her breath away. She needed something to drink as soon as possible.

"I really like your teacher, Brady Boe," Sasha commented.

I do too, thought Brady Boe.

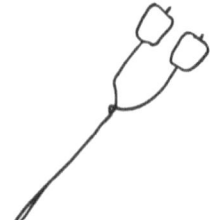

All Sasha could do when she got home was lie on the cool floor. Taylor decided to go home and rest up. They were all tired and hot. Brady Boe crashed on the couch after gulping down a glass of lemonade. Marcus on the hand was ready to play horsey with Sasha. He begged until Sasha gave in and gave him one ride. After a few minutes of resting, Brady Boe raced off to find Petunia. She wanted to show her the journal Mrs. Ramsey gave her. She found Petunia on the back patio working in the flower boxes.

"Look, Mom. Mrs. Ramsey gave us journals. We saw her on our way home."

Petunia examined the book Brady Boe held out. "Nice. I used to have a journal when I was a girl."

"Really?" Brady Boe was surprised. She always pictured her parents not having much of anything in their childhoods.

"Yes, really, dear. T-rex himself used to sit with me when I wrote in it," Petunia said jokingly. She knew the girls thought somehow that their parents were ancient.

Brady Boe laughed. "Mom, I know you didn't live in the dinosaur age. Mrs. Ramsey told us to write our life goals in it."

"Sounds like some good advice," Petunia lauded.

"I think I'm going to start writing in mine today." Brady Boe started to run off.

"Wait, Brady Boe. I almost forgot to tell you, Mrs. Windleton called. She wants to schedule to have her dog walked tomorrow morning at 9:00 am. If it's something you guys don't want to do, you will have to call her back."

Brady Boe thanked her mom for the message, but she knew to call and cancel an appointment with Mrs. Windleton was just a notion. They still needed twenty-five more dollars. Therefore, they would have to entertain Mrs. Windleton for now, she thought. Brady Boe decided to talk to Sasha about it later. She wanted to get to writing in her journal. Her best pen was waiting for her on her desk. The new blank page laid open for her to fill.

Dear Journal,

First things first, I will not let Mrs. Windleton scare me again. She is human just like me. I plan to be respectful, but firmly let her know she cannot speak to me any way she feels like it. I have a voice.

BB

Brady Boe stared at the words for a moment then closed her journal.

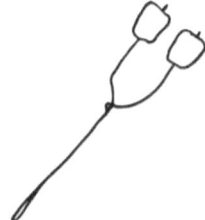

The next morning, Brady Boe was anxious to get started. She was up early with her dad before he went to work. Brady Boe told him about the journal Mrs. Ramsey had given them.

"Sounds like a good teacher to me," he said. He planted a kiss in the middle of her forehead before leaving for work.

Though Brady Boe told Sasha about going to Mrs. Windleton's that morning, Sasha was being difficult to get up and get going. Sasha asked a few times why they had to go when all she was going to do is be mean about it. Brady Boe did her best to convince her that every little bit of money helps.   She told Sasha not to worry she would do all the talking this time. Sasha sat upright in the bed.

"Well, I'm not going to miss that show. Sasha jumped out of bed and grabbed Brady Boe by the shoulders. "Are you feeling alright, Sister?"

"Yes, Sasha. I feel great. Let's get this done today."

"You are going to stand up to Mrs. Windleton today? ...because you know she always has a bad day."

"I don't know why you are making so much out of this. I can talk you know."

Sasha dashed around getting ready as fast as she could. She did not know what had come over Brady Boe, but she had to see this new attitude in action. Mrs. Windleton was the perfect candidate on which to practice. She did not care what she said to the girls. Brady Boe was outside practicing punching into the air when Sasha came out.

"Wow, you are serious, Sis."

"Come on, Sasha. Let's see if Taylor is ready."

"Don't we have to let mom know we are leaving?"

"I already did, Sasha." Brady Boe was getting irritated.

"Okay, relax already." Sasha pulled the door shut and ran to catch up with Brady Boe. She was already half-way across the street. Brady Boe did not hesitate. She knocked on the door. Taylor's mom answered and said Taylor was still in bed, but she would tell her that they came by. All the way to Mrs. Windleton's house, Brady Boe felt nervous about her proclamation. While Sasha rambled on about some dream she had, Brady Boe did her best to stay focused on her one goal that day: to refuse Mrs. Windleton the freedom to talk to her any kind of way. Every now and then, she felt Sasha's finger in her side asking her if she was paying attention. Brady Boe would just nod. Sasha would continue on talking.

At last, they stood before Mrs. Windleton's house. Brady Boe braced herself for what would go down in history. Sasha stopped talking about her dream and looked at Brady Boe staring at Mrs. Windleton's door.

"This is it, Brady Boe. You can do this. If you need me, I'll be right here. I practiced my southern accent last night, so I can say it with pizzazz."

Brady Boe flashed Sasha a nervous smile and looked down at her watch. They were right on time. They walked up the steps, and Brady Boe knocked on the door. Tiny barked on the other side of the door. They waited what seemed like forever. Brady Boe was about to knock again, but the door flew open with a gust. It made Sasha jump back.

"Tear my door down why don't you," growled Mrs. Windleton.

In their calmest voices, Brady Boe and Sasha said good morning. Mrs. Windleton ignored the greeting and went right into disciplining them for being a minute late. Sasha almost let it out, but she felt Brady Boe grab her arm.

"Take a lesson from your sister, Miss Sassy, and be quiet!"

Brady Boe's voice was shaking, but she managed to get the words out. "We were on time Mrs. Windleton. You didn't open the door until a minute after nine."

Mrs. Windleton's eyes darted at Brady Boe something furious. "Are you calling me a liar?"

"I am simply stating we were on time. I checked my watch."

Sasha looked pleased now.

"I will not have you keep Tiny waiting all morning for his walk. I have things to do, I'll have you know."

"Mrs. Windleton, we are here. Do you want us to walk Tiny or not?" Brady Boe could feel her blood rising to her face. She was surprised at how stern her words came out that time. It was not her intention to talk to Mrs. Windleton that way, but she kept pushing.

"How dare you rush me now child. You will just have to wait ten minutes while I get Tiny ready."

Mrs. Windleton started to close the door and Brady Boe raised her voice. "Wait, Mrs. Windleton!"

"I beg your pardon. I said sit there, and wait until I get Tiny ready!"

Brady Boe forgot about being nervous. Mrs. Windleton went too far this time. "No, Mrs. Windleton we will not wait, and we will not be back. We are done providing a service to you. You have not shown us any respect or courtesy in any way. Have a good day and don't, please don't I repeat, call us again!"

Sasha and Mrs. Windleton stood with their mouths wide-open watching Brady Boe march down the steps. Sasha turned to Mrs. Windleton and said, "Tell Tiny it's been fun." She, then, raced after Brady Boe.

Brady Boe was still revved up when Sasha caught up with her.

"Sasha, were those words really coming out of my mouth?"

"Yes, and they were beautiful, Brady Boe. It was like you were in a movie."

Brady Boe pointed to a nearby curb. "Let's sit over there for a minute, Sasha. I need to collect myself."

The girls sat on the curb in front of the community Pool house.

"Wow, I still can't believe you told her like it was."

"Oh no, Sasha. I feel almost sorry for her. Did you see how she looked before I walked away?"

"You didn't do anything wrong. You were totally respectful. That's what mom and dad always say. It's okay to say what you feel as long as you are being respectful."

"Great. What are we going to tell mom?"

"We'll just tell her that Mrs. Windleton changed her mind. She did... in a way."

"Thanks, Sasha. I'm glad you were with me."

"Don't worry, Sis. I'm always going to be here with you."

Brady Boe knew Sasha would want a hug, so she beat her to it. Sasha blushed and loved every bit of it.

When the girls arrived back at home, they told Petunia how much money they had and that they needed twenty-five more dollars. Petunia never asked why they were home so soon, and they did not volunteer any explanation. Just as they were all trying to think of more ways to get money for Margie, the phone rung and Mike came in belting, "Mail call!"

Sasha ran to answer the phone. "Hi, Margie."

Mike placed an envelope in front of Brady Boe on the table. Brady Boe looked suspicious.

"Go ahead open it," he urged.

"Brady Boe, I told Margie that we have not raised all the money yet. She wants to talk to you," hollered Sasha from the kitchen.

"Tell her to hold on, Sasha."

Brady Boe opened the envelope and green money bills fell out. It was exactly what they needed, twenty-five dollars. The girls cheered and thanked Mike with hugs and kisses.

"I like the attention, but don't thank me. Read the note."

Brady Boe looked puzzled. So did Petunia. She remembered the last letter Brady Boe got.

"Not that I wouldn't give you guys the money, but this wasn't from me," added Mike.

Brady Boe unfolded the paper and read the letter. "It's from Mrs. Ramsey! We were telling her about what we were doing to help Margie go to camp. How did she know what we needed?"

Petunia kissed Brady Boe's forehead, "She probably just followed her heart."

Brady Boe ran to the phone. "Margie, are you still there?"

"Yes," said Margie sounding a bit down.

"Margie, guess what?"

"What is it, Brady Boe? Sasha told me..."

Brady Boe could not let her finish. She waved Sasha over and whispered in her ear.

"Margie, guess what we are going to do?"

On the count of three Brady Boe and Sasha yelled, "WE ARE GOING TO CAMP!"

Chapter 5
Camp FireFly

The first day of Camp arrived, and Camp Firefly overflowed with kids and parents. Brady Boe, Sasha, and Taylor could hardly contain themselves. During the whole 15-mile ride to camp, they talked and laughed about what the week would bring. As soon as they arrived through the gates, the screams and giggles from Terra and Margie greeted them. At the entrance stood a huge Firefly statue. A group of workers dressed in the similar t-shirts and khaki shorts spread out to meet the campers and their families as they arrived. Two of them approached the group of girls, and introduced themselves as the camp counselors. They then offered to escort the girls to the check-in location. Marcus walked between Brady Boe and Sasha holding each of their hands. He skipped happily as they followed the counselors through the tree-lined, gravel path leading to a log cabin. Lots more people stood around socializing. Small kids darted around the adults playing and enjoying the outdoors.

While the parents checked in, the girls decided to wait outside and talk more about camp stuff. Terra's mom came out from checking in Terra and Margie. She said a quick good-bye and left. Margie was so excited. She must have said thank you a thousand times. Sasha finally told her not to say it again. Marcus was having a ball playing on a huge rock with a new friend he met. Mike and Petunia soon came out of the log cabin. A very peppy camp counselor approached them right away.

"Hi, my name is Miss Suzy Faye."

"Nice to meet you, Miss Suzy Faye. I'm Petunia Wells, and this is my husband Mike. I'm sure you will get acquainted with these girls real soon."

"Well, Mr. and Mrs. Wells I want to assure you that your girls will be perfectly safe here. I will be their personal counselor, and my cabin is right next to theirs. Each day we have a set of activities to keep them busy. I will also be doing checks throughout the day to make sure they are accounted for and enjoying themselves. We also have a set of rules that we stand strictly by. Number one being, stay with your group, even at meal times. I have a pep talk with the girls each morning when I do wake-up call. Would you two like to see the cabin they will be staying in?"

"Sure," said Petunia quite impressed at how Miss Suzy Faye said all those words without taking a breath.

Miss Suzy Faye asked the girls to gather around her. She introduced herself to them and made sure she had the correct cabin assignment for each of them. "Looks like all of four of you will be staying in the same cabin."

"Oh my goodness, guys," yelled Sasha creating another exciting frenzy among the girls.

Mike thanked them for giving his ears yet another shock. Miss Suzy Faye then led everyone through a path that led to their cabin. Along the way, she pointed out different buildings where they would participate in activities.

At last, they arrived in front of their cabin. Before entering, Miss Suzy Faye pointed out the signage and the number four on the cabin. "You girls will be in the Beetle group. The cabin number is four."

Petunia observed all the cabins around them. They were all small and similar. The colorful signs, each with a different insect name, were the only differences.

"I'd rather be a dragonfly," mumbled Sasha to Taylor, "They're much prettier."

A very basic floor plan characterized the inside of the cabin. Two sets of bunk beds against a wall, and a square mirror above a tiny sink on the opposite wall. In the corner of the room, a small bathroom nestled with a shower area separated by a heavy plastic curtain. The girls ran straight for the bunk beds each claiming the one she wanted. Miss Suzy Faye excused herself after giving the girls a set of rules to look over.

"Dinner will be at 5 o' clock sharp. I will be back at 4:30 to discuss the rules and escort you to the food hall. Feel free to unpack and settle in. You may go outside. Just don't leave this area until I come back again." Miss Suzy Faye started to leave, but turned back. "Oh, I almost forgot. You all will have to decide who will be responsible for the key." She handed the key to Terra who was standing near her. "There is a canteen across from your cabin. They have snacks and supplies if you need anything."

Petunia could see the excitement welling up at the mention of a canteen. She nudged Mike.

"I think this is a good time to leave."

Mike agreed and scooped Marcus up. "Say good-bye to your sisters," he instructed.

Marcus looked confused. Sasha ran up to him and planted a big kiss on his cheek. Brady Boe gave him a hi-five and told him she would get him something cool.

"Me don't want to go," he whined struggling to get down. Mike had a firm hold. He knew Marcus would react that way when it was time to go.

Petunia held her arms open to hug each of them. "Alright girls, promise to call me if you need anything, and remember to stay together."

"We will, Mommy," said Brady Boe.

"We are going to be fine, Mommy," assured Sasha.

Mike took hold of her hand and led her out the door. He knew it would be hard for her. They both worried in light of the black car incident and strange notes left. They did not want to make Brady Boe or Sasha paranoid. They just wanted them to have fun.

When the door closed behind her parents, Brady Boe thought they looked worried. She rather knew they would be. She assured herself that she and Sasha would have no problems. It would be a fun week for everyone.

After the girls unpacked their belongings, Terra suggested they all go over to the canteen for snacks.

"Sounds like a great idea to me," said Sasha snatching up her change purse.

The other three agreed as well and quickly scrambled around getting their money together. Right before heading out the door Terra handed Brady Boe the beaded necklace with the key attached.

"Here, you keep it, Brady Boe. You're the most responsible."

Brady Boe froze staring at the key, but more surprised by Terra's words. She knew Terra was a jokester.

"It's true, Brady Boe, she's right. Take the key," said Margie.

Brady Boe tried her hardest to think of something to say to change their mind, but she could not. Sasha finally said her piece to get Brady Boe past her frozen moment. "Come on, Sis. Just take it, and stop trying to think of a reason you shouldn't."

Brady Boe then took the key and put the beaded necklace around her neck. "We will discuss this later," she added pushing them out the door.

The canteen was camp paradise to the young girl's eyes. It had lots of different kinds of candies and an assortment of snacks. Every kind of drink, camp-themed crafts, and souvenirs surrounded them. The girls darted around exploring and excitedly pointing out things they found interesting to each other. After the girls concluded their shopping, they quickly headed back to their cabin to sort out all their goods. After a short time, Miss Suzy Faye showed up as promised.

Sasha took a liking to Miss Suzy Faye right away. She loved her upbeat personality and squeaky voice. Brady Boe knew Sasha was soaking it all up. She was sure she would hear some part of it later.

"So, do you girls have any questions about the rules?" She asked.

Terra looked at Margie. Margie looked at Brady Boe and Brady Boe looked at Taylor. Taylor nudged Sasha.

"Sorry, Miss Suzy Faye. We didn't read the rules yet," admitted Sasha.

"Well, that's okay, Sasha. I can take a few moments to go over them with you girls now."

The girls sat Indian style on the big circle rug to listen to Miss Suzy Faye. Miss Suzy Faye went down the list of rules explaining each one. She repeated rule number three twice noticing that Margie looked confused and the others started whispering amongst themselves.

"Rule number three: No sharing your marshmallows or chocolate. Keep it in your own graham crackers."

"I think we get it Miss Suzy Faye," said Terra quickly.

"All this talk about marshmallows and chocolate is making me hungry," Taylor said pretending to eat Sasha's arm.

"Alright, girls. Follow me. I'm going to lead you to the food hall where you will be eating all your meals while you're here," said Miss Suzy Faye.

Off through the woods they walked on the pebble rock path to the food hall. When they arrived, the place was buzzing with a multitude of kids talking all at once, apparently just as excited as they were to be there.

"Ryan," yelled Terra. "Over here."

Ryan made his way quickly from across the room. He brought a friend with him. Brady Boe thought he looked like Shane from the Jimmy Neutron cartoon.

"Hey, guys. This is my friend Alex."

Margie questioned Terra with her stare. Terra ignored her and kept talking to Ryan. Brady Boe noticed the whole interaction and leaned over to Margie. "Something is different about those two." Margie nodded in agreement.

When everyone had gone through the line and had their food, they sat in their assigned areas. Ryan and his friend Alex's assigned area just happened to be next to where the girls were sitting. Margie and Brady Boe watched as Terra and Ryan managed to sit right next to each other. Brady Boe decided to focus on something else besides Terra and Ryan. Terra definitely owed Margie and her an explanation later.

Sasha and Taylor seemed to have no problem making friends. Brady Boe thought Sasha looked quite at home chit chatting with the girls and boys sitting around her. Everyone enjoyed the tasty dinner that consisted of baked beans, hot dogs, cut-up raw veggies, and warm apple crisp. Brady Boe congratulated herself for saying thank you when a girl told her she like her purple t-shirt. She knew it was not as much as what Sasha would say, but at least she responded.

Miss Suzy Faye came over after a while to walk them back to their cabin. "Hey, girls. Let's head back so you can get rested for your busy, fun day tomorrow."

Sasha hugged her new friends and quickly ran to catch up with the others. As they walked through the pebbled path back, Margie tried to teach them a song from her home in Kosovo. They stumbled on the words she instructed. She finally gave up and told them to listen as she bellowed out the chorus as if she was in an opera. Even Miss Suzy Faye had to laugh. Though it was not fully dark yet, a few stars shined faint in the sky. The girls pulled out their flashlights and enjoyed using them to see their way back. Every now and then, they would flash each other in the face playfully.

That night Brady Boe so wanted to write in her journal, but she was too tired. It had been a good day. She would have to put it off until tomorrow. It was hard to go to sleep at first. Everyone was excited about what tomorrow would bring.

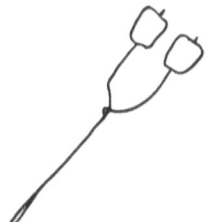

At breakfast, the food hall was full of hungry, noisy campers. The chatter filled every space in the room. Sasha and Taylor made conversation with the friends they made the night before. Brady Boe watched with wonder how comfortably Sasha talked with kids she did not know. She wondered if the ability lie in the fact that Sasha was not adopted. Sasha never had to question her identity, she thought. On the other hand, Brady Boe questioned who she really was. If only Iona had lived, she would have explained about her birth mom. She would have told Brady Boe why her birth mom did not want her anymore.

"Brady Boe! Where did you go? I have been asking you a question for the longest time." Margie appeared slightly irritated.

"Sorry, Margie. I was thinking about something."

"Obviously, Brady Boe, but I need you to look at our friend right now."

Brady Boe watched Terra and Ryan for a few minutes. They looked "pretty mushy" to her. She knew something was different. She just did not know how it got that way. She leaned over to Margie and whispered in her ear. "We are going to have to make her come clean, Margie." Margie seemed to like that, and displayed her eagerness.

"Let's do it, Brady Boe! Did you just see how he touched her hand?"

Brady Boe nudged Terra in her side with her elbow.

"What is it, Brady Boe? That was my side," whined Terra.

"I know. It seems to be the only way to get your attention. Margie and I would like some answers."

Terra tried to look clueless, but Margie just blurted out, "Are you and Ryan having an affair!?"

Brady Boe almost laughed aloud at Margie's words said with such passion. Terra looked strange for a moment. Then, she laughed hysterically. This triggered all the girls to laugh. Sasha stopped talking to her friend and asked, "What are we laughing about?"

Ryan and his friend Alex stared with a quirky look on their faces. When they all calmed down, Brady Boe leaned over and asked Terra. "Is it because you have marshmallows?"

Terra blushed immediately. "Brady Boe, what are you talking about?"

Margie quickly interjected before Brady Boe could answer. "We want to know what's going on between you two. You didn't act that way at school with him. As a matter of fact, you were kind of rude to him most of the time."

"She's right, Terra. So, what is it?"

Terra turn so Ryan could not see her face. "Alright. If you two must know, Ryan likes me."

Sasha decided to add her two cents. "And, you like him too. It's all over your face."

Terra rolled her eyes. "Whatever."

Miss Suzy Faye walked over at just the right time. Terra was relieved. She did not want to be the focus of the conversation any longer.

Miss Suzy Faye instructed the girls that it was time to go back to their cabin for an hour and a half rest period before she took them to the swimming hole.

"Yay!" yelled Sasha and Taylor.

On the walk back, Brady Boe and Margie attempted to interrogate Terra more about her feelings for Ryan, but she refused to tell them more. They let her off the hook until later.

The swimming hole was a lake next to the camping quarters of Camp Firefly. It featured a wooden deck that stretched out into the water. Bright orange sponges bobbed some distance out in the water to mark where the boundaries were. After going over the swimming rules, Miss Suzy Faye told the girls to have fun before going to sit with the other camp counselors.

Sasha and Taylor wasted no time. They raced to the edge of the deck and jumped off, creating a big splash when they hit the water. Other campers were splashing too and having fun playing water games. Margie noticed Terra looking around anxiously.

"So, you're looking for Ryan huh? Well, I'm not sticking around for that scene. Are you coming, Brady Boe?"

"Don't go, Brady Boe, begged Terra. I really want to talk to you."

Brady Boe hesitated. She hated feeling torn between her two friends. "Oh okay, Terra. Go ahead, Margie. I'll find you in a minute."

Terra had a silly grin on her face as she pulled Brady Boe over to a part of the deck where fewer kids were.

"Brady Boe, don't say anything until you hear me out. Promise?"

Brady Boe agreed with a nod.

"Ryan's friend Alex likes you."

"What!" exclaimed Brady Boe. He doesn't even know me!"

"He wants to talk to you. What do you think, Brady Boe?"

"Really, Terra? What do I think?"

"Well, just think about it. I'm just going to warn you. He may try to talk to you."

"No, Terra. I'm not ready for that."

Sasha swam up. "Come on, Brady Boe. Jump in!"

Brady Boe looked at Terra as she answered Sasha. "Why not, Sasha. That is why we came to camp to have fun with each OTHER!"

Terra spotted Ryan and Alex across the way and waved for them to come over. Brady Boe made a big splash into the water and swam as far as she could to get away from Terra.

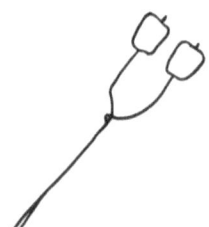

That night everyone was exhausted. After swimming most of the day, eating dinner, and hanging out in the game room, they could barely keep their eyes open once they got back to the cabin. Brady Boe had a lot to write in her journal. She turned on her little flashlight after crawling under her blanket.

Dear Journal,

First, I must admit, I miss mommy, daddy, and Marcus. I am having a blast though even if Terra is soo focused on Ryan. I 'm glad I got to come to camp. I think it would be cool to work here one day, like Miss Suzy Faye.

Something crazy happened today. Terra told me that Ryan's friend Alex likes me. How could that be? I don't want to be like Terra thinking she needs to be around Ryan every minute of the day. I don't even like boys like that yet! I guess it would be kind of cool having someone like you, but I don't want to be all mushy like them, we could just play games together or something. I hope Sasha doesn't find out. She would never let me forget that someone likes me. My goal is to figure out me first before I start liking boys like Terra. Good night!

Chapter 6
The Heart Wants…

"Pancake day," yelled Sasha! She and Taylor were the first ones up and dressed. Margie dragged out of her sleeping bag slowly while Brady Boe was the next to stretch and come alive. Terra lay in her bunk deep in thought.

The food hall would be open soon, and Sasha could hardly wait. Pancakes and sausage were on the menu, and she was starving. Taylor pulled her arm.

"Come on, Sasha. Let's go outside and wait. Maybe we will see some of our friends."

Sasha did not need much convincing. She turned to follow Taylor out the door.

Brady Boe yelled behind them. "Don't go far!"

She actually sounded concerned yelling out like that. The truth was she did not think there was a reason to worry. She did not see how anything could go wrong. Margie decided to wait outside too. The sun had come up, and other kids were hanging outside waiting on their camp counselors to come and escort them to breakfast.

Terra seem not herself that morning. She finally rolled out of bed.

66

"What's going on with you, Terra?" asked Brady Boe. "This is a drastic mood switch from yesterday?"

"I need to ask you something, Brady Boe."

Brady Boe looked concerned, hoping Terra was not about to mention Alex again. "Alright, what is it?"

"Do you really think Ryan really likes me?" Terra stumbled over words, which was not like her at all.

"Yesterday at the swimming hole, I heard some girls say Ryan only liked me because of my marshmallows."

Brady Boe was in a state of shock. She could not imagine being so distraught over some boy, especially Ryan. She searched for something to tell Terra. She looked so upset.

"Brady Boe! I really need your help."

Brady Boe thought about what Sasha would say at this moment, and braced herself to let Terra have it.

"Terra, look at you. You're sitting here at camp where we should be having fun. Instead, you are worrying yourself over a boy who used to annoy you to death. Of course, he likes you for your marshmallows. He's a boy isn't he?"

"I can't help that I have marshmallows, Brady Boe. When you get some, then you'll understand."

Brady Boe looked down at her shirt. Then, she focused back on Terra. "Look, Terra. Ryan acts like he likes you. I think only time will tell why he really likes you. But for the record, if having marshmallows makes you act like that, I don't want them!"

"Brady Boe, you are the only one I can talk to. I don't think Margie will understand. I have one more thing to tell you."

Brady Boe could not handle anymore from Terra.

"I think I like him too. Don't tell anyone I told you that. Promise, Brady Boe."

Brady Boe could not believe Terra. "You think you like him, Terra. Let me know when you are sure of it."

There was a knock at the door. Miss Suzy Faye came in.

"Time to get some grub, girls."

Brady Boe was glad for the save and hurried out the door ignoring Terra's stern stare.

After breakfast, Miss Suzy Faye offered the girls a choice as to which craft activity they wanted to participate. Sasha and Taylor chose the bracelet making class. Brady Boe, Margie, and Terra chose the art class. Sasha ran over to Brady Boe right before they spilt up into groups.

"Brady Boe, be safe okay. I don't want anything happening to my big sis." Sasha gave Brady Boe a quick hug before she could refuse.

Brady Boe started to tell Sasha she was making too big of a deal about something happening, but decided to leave it alone. Sasha was just showing she cared. She let her slide this one time. Besides, she thought, no black cars were coming all the way out here to camp. Brady Boe appreciated Sasha for caring. Sometimes she thought Sasha was too busy being friendly with other kids to care about her. Any other time Brady Boe would try to wiggle free or tell Sasha to keep it down, but this time she wanted others to know that she was her big sister and she cared about her. She wanted others to know about their relationship as sisters.

"Don't worry, Sasha. No black car can come out here in the woods without someone seeing it."

"I guess you're right, Brady Boe. Have fun in your art class. Make something really pretty!"

That must have satisfied Sasha because she quickly ran over to her group and picked up talking where she left off with Taylor and another girl who was standing with them.

In the art class Margie, Terra, and Brady Boe sat together. Ryan and Alex were nearby of course because Terra would not have it any other way. The art class took place outside under a picnic pavilion.

Nearby was a bird feeder tower and a squirrel who frequently climbed it robbing the birds of their seeds. Brady Boe was glad the class was outside where she could look away and focus on something other than Terra and Ryan. The counselors passed around supplies, which consisted of one thin 8x12 canvas, two paintbrushes, one small cup of water, and an empty egg carton cut in half for each person. Each table shared an array of paint colors. Campers were instructed to create a picture from the nature scene around them.

Brady Boe chose to focus her attention on a nearby Blue Jay that seemed to be interested in something inside a bush. Margie decided to paint a picture of a lonely wild flower situated on the edge of the woods. Terra was still undecided. Margie took the opportunity to tell her why.

Brady Boe sat between Margie and Terra. When Margie leaned in to talk to Terra, Brady Boe had to hear it.

"Terra, you can't draw Ryan for your picture."

"Ha Ha, Margie. Very funny!"

"I just thought I'd let you know, he's not part of the nature scene."

"I wasn't even thinking about it, Margie. Do you hear her, Brady Boe?"

Brady Boe just hunched her shoulders in reply. She really did not want to be caught in the middle of their teasing and deflection. The talk with Terra that morning was draining enough. Though she would not dare say it aloud, she sided with Margie. However, that should not be a secret to Terra. Margie was more like Sasha but with less self-confidence. Sasha was sure of herself where Margie hoped what she said mattered.

"Don't bring Brady Boe into this, Terra. The reason you can't draw anything is because you're too busy making googly eyes at Ryan."

Margie's comment made them all laugh.

"Margie, I know what your problem is. You want a boyfriend too. Don't worry. I'll find you one," teased Terra.

"Oh, no thanks. I'm not interested." Margie looked at Brady Boe for assurance. "Is that the way to say it, Brady Boe?"

"Yes. That covers it, Margie." Brady Boe glanced at Ryan and Alex wondering if they heard anything of the girls' conversation. They seemed to be having their own issues at the moment. Ryan appeared to be having a rather intense conversation with Alex. He was using many hand movements when he talked.

Terra finally took the paintbrush and made a few strokes on her canvas. "This is my picture of grass. How do you guys like it?"

Miss Suzy Faye came around and examined the girls' paintings. She stopped to look at Terra's.

"I think it needs a sun and a sky at least."

Margie was pleased with Miss Suzy Faye's comments for Terra and started back working on her own picture.

Brady Boe was relieved that the spat was over. She wanted to finish her Blue Jay, but Terra had other plans.

"Look, Brady Boe." Terra unfolded a piece of paper and showed it to Brady Boe.

Brady Boe stared at the paper puzzled at first. It did not look like anything Terra would write to her. She read the note.

Will you be my girlfriend?
Circle yes or no

Brady Boe grabbed the note from Terra and was about to circle no after realizing Ryan wrote it to Terra. Terra snatched it back and circled yes before passing the note back to Ryan. A big smile came over Ryan's mouth as he and Terra exchanged looks. Brady Boe knew what the discussion would be about tonight in their cabin. Margie choose to ignore Brady Boe and Terra for the moment though she knew something was going on.

Terra handed Brady Boe another folded piece of paper.

"No, Terra. You already circled yes. Why do I need to see it again?"

"You have to read this one, Brady Boe," begged Terra. "Please think about it before you answer."

Brady Boe took the note and gave her a cross look. She hoped it was not what she thought it was. After reading the note, it was exactly what she thought it was a note from Alex.

Hi Brady Boe. I like you a lot.
Will you be my girlfriend?
Circle yes or no

Brady Boe ignored the whispering she heard in the background and circled no before handing the note back to Terra.

"Brady Boe, you didn't even think about it!"

"I did to. Besides, what is there to think about, Terra?"

Once again, Miss Suzy Faye saved the day. This time telling them to pack up their things so they could go to lunch. On the way, Brady Boe filled Margie in on the note Alex had given her. Margie congratulated her on being strong.

"Now, we can't go on a double date," added Terra.

"What would your mom and dad say about all of this, Terra," asked Margie feeling like Terra was going too far with the dating thing.

"Sometimes, I wish I was adopted. Then, I wouldn't have to worry about what they thought. They wouldn't care what I did."

Brady Boe felt the color go out of her face. Margie was beginning to get real annoyed with Terra.

"Terra, that was not a nice thing to say!"

"I was just joking, Margie."

Though Terra was just joking, her words disturbed Brady Boe. Could it be that adoptive parents cared less for the kids they adopted? She was already wondering if her birth mom cared anything about her. Now, she had to think about Mike and Petunia too. Brady Boe really wanted to get away from Terra at that moment.

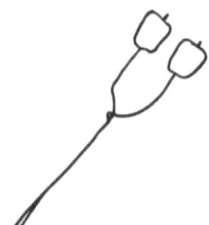

Brady Boe was glad to get back to the cabin. She needed to write in her journal. Margie must have sensed something was wrong with her because she stopped her before she went inside.

"Are you alright, Brady Boe? When Terra made that joke about wishing she was adopted, you didn't like it either, huh?"

Brady Boe managed to respond, "No, it wasn't very funny. I'll be fine. Don't worry, Margie."

Sometimes Brady Boe wished she could tell her friends that she was adopted. But, now she was glad she didn't. She felt that she would be the butt of all Terra's jokes, if she had told.

A moment later, Sasha and Taylor came charging through the door full of excitement. "Hey, girls. I bring gifts for each of you!" Yelled Sasha. Sasha pulled bracelets from her bag. She had one for each of them except Brady Boe.

"These are so nice," praised Margie. "Thank you."

"Thanks, Sasha," said Terra putting hers on right away.

"Brady Boe, I made you a special one. See." Sasha held up the bracelet for everyone to see. It featured beads in the shape of hearts that were fluorescent in a variety of colors.

"It glows in the dark. Do you like it, Brady Boe?"

Brady Boe took the bracelet from Sasha. "I love it, Sasha. Thank you!"

"Really, sis?"

"Yes, really, Sasha."

Sasha threw her arms around Brady Boe and held her tight.

"Sasha, I can't breathe."

"Aww, too sweet. Group hug everyone!" Yelled Margie.

Everyone huddled in until they all ended up on the floor. Brady Boe was glad Sasha was there with her. She felt better already.

Taylor changed the topic. "Did anyone hear what is going to happen tonight?"

"No, is it a surprise?" Asked Terra.

"Miss Suzy Faye is taking us to a huge bonfire!" Screamed Taylor. "We are going to make S'mores and sing songs around the fire. I'm surprised she didn't tell you guys."

"I guess you're special," said Terra sarcastically.

"That will be perfect, Brady Boe. You can wear your glow in the dark bracelet," Sasha suggested.

"S'mores are my favorite summer treat," said Taylor.

"Will all the campers be there?" Asked Terra.

"I wonder why you want to know that," Margie said with sarcasm.

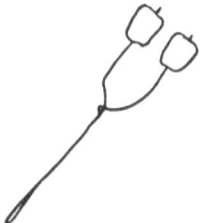

The night could not come fast enough now that the girls knew about the bonfire event. At dinner, the hall buzzed with excitement concerning the bonfire. Terra could not wait to tell Ryan, so they could sit together.

Margie nudged Brady Boe. "Terra is really starting to gross me out with how she is acting about Ryan."

"I know, Margie, but I don't know if there is anything we can do about it. Ryan has her under his spell."

"Well, I'm not going to worry about her tonight. I just want to have fun at the bonfire."

"I'm glad we all got a chance to come to camp together, even if Terra is acting strange over Ryan. It's been fun," said Brady Boe feeling most grateful for achieving the goal of getting Margie there.

In her cheerleader voice Miss Suzy Faye yelled, "Alright, girls! We are going to head back to your cabins for just a bit. Then, it will be BONFIRE TIME!"

The announcement got everybody excited. When they arrived back at their cabins, no one stayed inside. They hung outside talking and running about with flashlights. When it was just about dark, Miss Suzy Faye reappeared. Miss Suzy Faye led the way down the pebbly path to the area where the bonfire would take place.

A huge fire was already blazing high at the bonfire spot. Nearby, S'more fixings sat atop a picnic table. Logs stood at the ready near the fire to throw in as needed. Larger logs were arranged around the fire for the campers to sit upon. By the fire, sat two counselors. One had a guitar, and the other, who resembled Miss Suzy Faye except her voice was squeakier, sang to the music. Sasha Immediately ran up front and jumped right in singing and swaying.

Brady Boe shook her head. How bold, she thought. She then headed over to the table to do something she did well, eat s'mores.

Terra was content to be sitting right next Ryan as they waved their marshmallows over the fire. Brady Boe saw Alex sitting with them. She felt almost sorry for him trying to be a part of whatever it was they had. He looked awkward as he tried to be included.

It was the perfect night. The stars were bright in the sky and everyone was having a good time. Brady Boe and Margie joined in the singing while eating their s'mores. Brady Boe decided that she could handle one more. While not many kids were at the table, she made a run for it. While gathering the fixings for her s'more, a counselor she was not familiar with approached her.

"Are you, Brady Boe?" He asked.

Brady Boe said a slow "yes" feeling she was caught getting her second s'more.

"Your mom is at the office. She said you forgot something that you would need tonight. If you follow that path right there," he said pointing to wooded path nearby. "It will take you straight to the office."

Brady Boe looked puzzled and started to speak.

"Look, I know you are having a good time, but you shouldn't leave your mom waiting. You'll be back in no time."

Brady Boe froze. She did not know what to do. Was Petunia there, or was this just a joke? She must have hesitated too long because the counselor looked impatient and mean now.

Brady Boe did not want to upset him any further, so she started for the path. She looked back to try and see Sasha, but she could not spot her right away. She walked slow hoping the counselor would get busy doing something else so she could pretend as if she went and came back. But, her thoughts kept telling her what if it was Petunia really there. Why would he lie? Maybe Petunia just missed her and wanted to see her.

Sasha was busy talking with Taylor when she happened to look up and see Brady Boe headed for the wooded path alone. Her glow in the dark bracelet gave her away. Sasha immediately stopped what she was doing and ran after Brady Boe.

"Brady Boe, wait!" Yelled Sasha.

Taunya S. Wright

Brady Boe turned around quickly relieved to hear Sasha's voice.

When Sasha caught up to her, she asked, "Where are you going, Brady Boe?"

"To the office, one of the counselors said mom was at the office to give me something I would need tonight. I asked him if he was sure it was my mom, but he kept telling me to go."

"I don't know if that's right, Brady Boe. Why would mom bring you anything at this time though?"

"I don't know either, Sasha. The only thing I can think of is maybe she really misses us and just wants to make sure we are okay. You know how she worries and all."

"Yeah, you are right. Mom does worry about us, but it still seems strange."

Brady Boe and Sasha walked a little further down the path. They now had the office in their view. Brady Boe jerked her head around, "Sasha, did you hear that?"

Sasha whispered back, "Yes, what was it?"

"It sounded like someone stepping on some crunchy leaves."

"Brady Boe, you are creeping me out." Sasha could feel her heart beginning to beat faster.

Brady Boe grabbed Sasha's hand. "Whatever happens, Sasha, stay with me."

"Okay, Brady Boe," Sasha looked around. "I don't see mom, Brady Boe."

Suddenly the girls heard what sounded like a radio or someone talking on a walkie-talkie. The voices were conversing back and forth, "Have you seen her yet? Hurry up we don't have a lot of time here."

"There's two of them."

"Darn, just grab them both and hurry before somebody knows they are missing!"

Brady Boe and Sasha froze in their steps not wanting to make any noise.

"Did you hear that, Brady Boe," whispered Sasha as low as she could? "That doesn't sound like mom at all waiting on us."

"I did, Sasha. We are going to have to run. Don't let go of my hand for nothing. Ok, let's run!"

As soon as the girls took off through the woods, they could hear footsteps behind them. Heavy footsteps. Brady Boe did her best to dodge twigs that were dangling from the low hanging branches.

"It's so dark, Brady Boe. I can't see anything," yelled Sasha!

Brady Boe yelled back, "It doesn't matter, Sasha. We can't let them catch us. Just scream Sasha as loud as you can!"

The steps behind them seemed to be gaining on them. "HELP!" Screamed Sasha over and over again. Brady Boe held her hand tight. Her legs were getting tired and she had no clue where she was going she just knew she could not stop. Sasha felt like she was being dragged, but she was not about to complain. She did not know her sister could run so fast.

Brady Boe's heart was pounding. She kept thinking how could she be so dumb to think Petunia was waiting at the office. Now she has put Sasha's life in danger along with her own. Brady Boe almost lost Sasha's hand leaping over a small limb, but Sasha held on. Sasha kept looking back, she could see the outline of a figure, but she could not see the face. The person had on a mask, and it was dark.

"Brady Boe, whoever it is he is still chasing us. It looks like he is getting tired."

"Just keep running and screaming Sasha," ordered Brady Boe. Somebody from the camp has to hear us, she thought.

"Help, help!"

A few moments later Brady Boe and Sasha saw lights flickering in the distance. Brady Boe thought she heard the faint sound of her name being called. They ran in the direction of the voices. Their pursuer stopped when he saw the flashlights and headed back in the opposite direction.

Soon the girls were staring Miss Suzy Faye in the face.

"Girls, are you okay?"

They were so out of breath they could only point in the direction behind them. Three male counselors took off running in the direction where they pointed.

Sasha finally caught her breath. "What took you guys so long?!"

Miss Suzy Faye apologized repeatedly all the way back to the camp. On their way, Brady Boe noticed the sound of tires quickly spinning through the gravel of the parking lot. Whoever was trying to catch her and Sasha must have been in the car. It hurried away as soon as the counselors approached the parking lot at the edge of the woods.

Miss Suzy Faye decided to take the girls to the manager's cabin office to sort out what had happened. When they arrived, she offered them a seat on the couch. Sasha was still hanging on to Brady Boe. Brady Boe could feel her trembling. They both were wet from sweating. Miss Suzy Faye wrapped a blanket around them, lit a candle, and took a seat in a chair across form them.

"Girls, please tell me what happened to you to…"

Sasha interrupted before Miss Suzy Faye could finish. "What happened to the lights?"

"I don't know Sasha. We have experienced a power outage. Our phones are out too, but do not worry, we will have it looked at in the morning. I'm just glad you two are alright. Did anyone hurt either of you?"

"No," answered Brady Boe, "but my legs are really tired."

"I bet they are, Brady Boe. You are a real trooper for how you took care of your sister out there."

Sasha rolled her eyes. Brady Boe knew that meant Sasha was irritated and Miss Suzy Faye was getting ready to get a piece of her mind. Brady Boe committed to intervene.

"We don't need your compliments right now. Our life was in serious danger all because that one counselor told me to go to the office to get something from my mom in the middle of us having a bonfire. He didn't even go with me!"

Miss Suzy Faye looked scared. Sashed looked impressed and added, "What she said."

"Don't worry, girls. Counselor Chris will receive a reprimand and will not be back. He should have checked with me before sending you anywhere. I am truly sorry. "

The door to the office opened and the three guy counselors including the one who sent Brady Boe to the office walked in.

"We couldn't get whoever it was," said the tallest counselor. Counselor Chris looked at Brady Boe and Sasha nervously and did not say a word.

"Which one was it, Brady Boe, that told you mom was at the office," blurted out Sasha. Sasha was upset and the fact that they did not catch anyone made her even madder.

Brady Boe pointed to the nervous looking counselor. Counselor Chris started to explain, but Miss Suzy Faye stopped him.

"Chris, what you did was outside protocol. These girls could have been hurt. In the morning, we will write all this up and discuss it with the camp supervisor."

Counselor Chris nodded and did not attempt to say anything else.

Sasha was surprised to hear Miss Suzy speak that sternly. She did not know she had it in her.

Miss Suzy Faye and one of the other counselors walked the girls to their cabin. She told them to lock the door and not to let anyone one in for any reason. "You will be safe tonight, and I will see you bright and early in the morning," she assured them.

Taylor, Terra and Margie had plenty of questions for Brady Boe and Sasha. Brady Boe told them they got lost without elaborating on the details. Somehow, they knew that was all the information they were going to get and did not press any further. Margie hugged Brady Boe, "I'm glad you're okay."

Brady Boe appreciated that and pulled out her flashlight to see her way to the bathroom to clean herself up.

Sasha refused to sleep alone. She cuddled up next to Brady Boe. "If I could, Brady Boe, I'd walk home tonight."

"I know, Sasha. I'm just glad you're safe."

"Good night, Brady Boe."

"Good night, Sasha."

Chapter 7
Questions for Lily

The morning light shown through the little cabin window. Brady Boe yawned and stretched. Sasha was still asleep. So was everyone else. Last night's events streamed through her mind. She wondered what that guy would have done if he had caught them. All she wanted to do was come to camp and have fun. Now, her mom and dad will have to know what happened. They may never trust her again. Everyone slowly awakened, and they all started getting ready. The power was still out but they had some light from the window to see by.

Taylor dashed out of the shower. "It's kind of strange taking a shower in the dark."

"I wonder if the power will be on soon. I really would like to wash my hair and use my blow dryer," whined Terra.

Margie made the motion of zipping her lip, while rolling her eyes at Terra's statement. She knew Ryan probably had something to do with it.

Soon all of them had experienced the dark shower feeling. They dressed quickly ready to get out of the cabin as soon as they could. Miss Suzy Faye arrived early as promised. "How did you girls manage this morning?"

Terra took the opportunity to gripe about the power being out, not having enough hot water for her shower, and her hunger because she did not get a chance to eat another s'more before they were all rushed back to their cabins last night. Miss Suzy Faye held up her hand to stop Terra from adding to the list.

"Well, the power company is here, and the power should be restored soon. Great news is we have a generator for the breakfast hall so you should have a hot breakfast this morning. Alright, girls. Let's head out!"

"Sounds good to me. I'm starving," said Taylor grabbing Sasha's hand.

"Brady Boe and Sasha, can I talk to you for a moment? You girls go ahead. We are right behind you."

Brady Boe and Sasha stayed behind to walk with Miss Suzy Faye. "I just wanted to let you girls know that we had to let Counselor Chris go this morning. We are also going to let your parent's know what happened. My supervisor will talk to them as soon as we get the power back on. "Did you girls sleep okay?"

"I just want to know what color was the car that zoomed off in the parking lot?" Asked Sasha rather bluntly and ignoring Miss Suzy Faye's question.

"It was too dark to really tell Sasha. We do not have a lot of information on who it was or what the car looked like. I really want you girls to enjoy your last day here, so if there is something you want, just let me know."

They both nodded and Miss Suzy Faye lagged behind to make sure the kids behind them kept up. More counselors were visible Brady Boe noticed.

Right before entering the food hall, Sasha pulled Brady Boe aside. "Do you think the guy that was chasing us last the same person that was chasing us in the black car on our way home from school before?"

Brady Boe hesitated, "Sasha I...think it might be my birth mother. I think she really misses me or wants me back."

"Why would she scare us like that, Brady Boe. It just doesn't seem like the thing to do?"

"I don't know, Sasha. Maybe she just doesn't know what to do."

"Why didn't she just keep you in the first place?" Sasha spoke with so much anger it startled Brady Boe.

Brady Boe did her best to choke back the tears that threatened to appear. "I don't know, Sasha."

They turned and walked into the food hall both feeling disturbed.

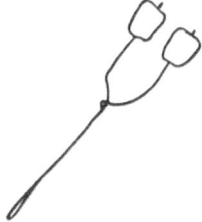

At home, things were quieter without the Brady Boe and Sasha running around. Everyday Marcus faithfully would wake up and run into each of the girl's room calling their names. Petunia and Mike took turns telling him that the girls would be home soon. The morning was going great until Petunia went out to get the mail. When she got back in Mike questioned the look on her face.

"What happened? You look like you've seen a ghost."

Petunia handed Mike an envelope. It was addressed to Petunia with no return address. Mike looked confused.

"Turn it over," instructed Petunia.

Mike turned it over and read the name written where the envelope was sealed. "Lily P. Hayes," he said aloud.

Petunia had a worried look on her face. "What could she want, Mike?"

Mike took Petunia's hand and led her to the couch where they both sat. "Well, let's see."

Mike opened the envelope and unfolded the letter. He held it where they could both read it. After reading the contents of the letter, they both sat back in shock. She was glad the girls were at camp.

"So, I'm thinking if she wants to see Brady Boe so bad, why didn't she come to the last meeting that was set up to do that?"

"You have a point Petunia. In this letter, she certainly refers to herself as the loving mother who made one mistake. Which, in my opinion, we gave her a chance to at least meet Brady Boe.," explained Mike.

"She's probably feeling guilty, which I understand. The thing that worries me is if she is stalking Brady Boe...Brady Boe shouldn't have to go through that is what I'm trying to say."

"I agree totally. I support you honey. I'll do whatever you want to do. Do you want to meet with her?" Asked Mike.

"I feel like we should, Mike. Not for her to meet Brady Boe, but to tell her to back off. Brady Boe is loved and safe. Lily had a chance to connect. Now, she needs to live with her choice."

Petunia could feel herself losing it. "You know, Mike, ever since we told Brady Boe that she's adopted I've been thinking more about my own adoption. My birth mom never tried to contact me. What if Brady Boe wants her? I just don't want to lose Brady Boe."

Mike took Petunia in his arms. "If you are not up to this, you don't have to do it. But, I want you to know that no one is going to take Brady Boe away from us. I won't let them. She wants to meet with you. I say meet with her while the girls are at camp. We need to know what her intentions are."

"Mike, do you think it was her chasing the girls in the black car on their way home from school?"

"I don't know, Petunia. We really don't have any evidence, but if it turns out that it was her, we need to take legal action."

"She says the father never agreed to the adoption, and now he wants to see Brady Boe."

"Well, that's not going to happen! He is not our problem. All the more reason to end this mess!" Mike threw the letter onto the table. "Let's call her bluff."

Petunia knew that when Mike made up his mind it was final. She picked up the letter and called the number written in it. Petunia noticed her hands trembling while holding the phone. Mike paced up one side and down the other side of the room. Petunia hated that Lily P. Hayes resurfaced in their lives. Ms. Iona was such a sweet and calm person. If she were still alive, she would not have minded Brady Boe visiting her. But something seemed eerie about Lily. Something she could not put her finger on. Why had she waited to see Brady Boe? she questioned to herself. Finally, someone answered the line. Petunia scribbled an address on a nearby pad on the table. "I understand," she said talking to the person on the other side of the line. "This will be our last time attempting to meet you." Petunia then hung up.

Mike embraced Petunia. "I know this is difficult for you, but we are going to get through this. So, when does the show start?"

"At noon, at the Deer Park over on 21st street. She wants Brady Boe there."

"What she wants right now is not my concern. I'm concerned about her intentions concerning Brady Boe," said Mike slightly irritated. The fact that Lily mentioned the father made him suspicious.

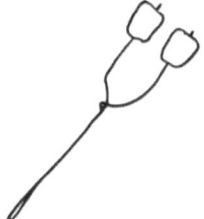

At camp, it was hard to concentrate on anything that day. The events of the night before kept interfering in Brady Boe's thoughts. The girls went to a craft making class to learn how to make glass coasters and potholders. Brady Boe could tell Sasha was still angry by the way she intentionally fixed her gaze away from her. ` Margie knew something was going on between Brady Boe and Sasha and did her best to bring them together again, but her efforts failed. Sasha just ignored her and pouted. Brady Boe brushed her off telling her it would be okay. Brady Boe just wanted to go back to the cabin and write. She felt so torn inside.

Miss Suzy Faye hovered close. She noticed that Brady Boe seemed disengaged from the craft projects.

"Brady Boe, is there something wrong?"

Brady Boe hesitated for a moment before she answered. "No, I just don't want to make anything. I want to write in my journal."

The statement caused Sasha look up for a moment, but when she saw Brady Boe look in her direction, she quickly turned away.

"Well, I guess that should be okay. Just stay near us where I can see you."

Miss Suzy Faye's response pleased Brady Boe. She rummaged around in her backpack and pulled out her journal. Brady Boe found a nice grassy spot where she was still in Miss Suzy's Faye's view and settled into writing.

Brady Boe concluded that she needed a plan. Besides the near death experience last night with her and Sasha, she also woke up to something disturbing. When she looked in the mirror, she noticed marshmallows had appeared on her chest. They were not very noticeable, but they were present. Her first thought was that Terra had something to do with this. She soon dismissed the idea through disbelief that Terra could be that powerful. Terra did want Brady Boe to like Alex, but she would not go to those measures, she thought. A talk with Petunia will be her first step, she decided. In her journal, she had to figure out what she wanted to know from her birth mom. When she knew it, she could stop hurting those around her. Brady Boe wrote six questions down in her journal.

1. *Why did you give me up?*
2. *Do you love me?*
3. *Did you give me up because I had a fatal disease?*
4. *Did you want a boy?*
5. *What is wrong with me?*
6. *Are you the one in the black car trying to get me? If so, please stop because you are scaring my family.*

Brady Boe felt satisfied with her questions. Once she knew the answers, she figured she could move on with her life. The only problem was how to get those answers.

Terra ranted on and on about what she and Ryan were going to do once they got back home. Taylor chatted with some new friends. Margie was really into making her potholder. Sasha was set on being gloomy. Soon, it would be time to go home. Brady Boe did not want camp to end on a sad note for Sasha. The incident last night was the only interruption of their fun.

When the craft time concluded, Miss Suzy Faye escorted everyone back to their cabins. Brady Boe stopped Sasha before she went in.

"How long are you going to be mad, Sasha?"

Sasha turned up her nose. "Until you admit you want to go with your birth mom."

"Sasha, why would I admit that?"

"Because you are always trying to go with her. You think about her all the time. That's why she keeps chasing us!"

"That is not true, Sasha, I am not trying to go with anyone! We don't even know for sure if that was her chasing us. I've never seen her." Brady Boe did not quite know how to address the accusation of thinking about her birth mom all the time. It was not all the time, in her mind.

"Look, Sasha. I just want some answers. I came up with a plan."

This intrigued Sasha. "What's your plan, Brady Boe?"

"Well, don't get too excited. It's just a list of questions I want answered by my birth mom. Then, I don't have to wonder anymore. The only thing is finding a way to ask her."

"So, you don't want to leave us?"

"No, Sasha. I never said I wanted to leave."

Sasha lunged in and squeezed Brady Boe so tightly that Brady Boe could hardly wiggle free.

"Oh, sister. I was mad for nothing. I'm sorry."

"It's okay, Sasha."

"Brady Boe, I don't think we should tell mom and dad about what happened last night. They would just worry themselves to death."

"You're probably right, but Miss Suzy Faye has to tell them. I don't think there's any way of getting around it."

"I guess the best part is that we are safe," said Sasha.

"Yeah, I agree. Now, let's have some fun our last few hours of camp!"

Brady Boe liked that Sasha was back to her old self again. Life was good again.

Over the PA system, a voice announced that the power had been restored, but the phone service was still down and being worked on. The campers cheered from their different locations. They flipped on the lights in their cabins in awe as if it was their first time experiencing it.

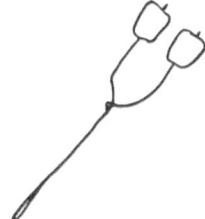

At home, Petunia and Mike prepared to go to Deer Path Park. Marcus, excited about the idea, asked repeatedly if "Boe and Sasha," would be there.

Deer Path Park was about a twenty-minute drive from their home. It sat nestled in a shady area of downtown Nashville. Petunia and Mike rode in silence most of the way there, both lost in their thoughts about what was about to happen.

When they arrived, Mike parked in a lot close to the park. Marcus had practically gotten himself out of his car seat in a rush to go play. "Swing," he screeched viewing the playground from his position in the car. Mike and Petunia did a quick scan of the park. It appeared they were the only ones there besides a couple of teens horsing around on the jungle gym.

Mike followed Marcus over to the swings. They kept occupied playing with Marcus as he ran from one piece of equipment to the next. Ten minutes had passed, and Mike looked down at his watch. "She's late."

"This is starting to remind me of another time," added Petunia.

More time had passed and no sign of Lily. Petunia was somewhat disappointed. She wanted to ask Lily a few things. "No use waiting any longer. We tried."

"I mean it, Petunia. I'm not playing anymore of her games. No more trying to meet. Clearly, she had no intention of showing up. What if Brady Boe was with us? She would be disappointed all over again."

Petunia knew that Mike was right. Brady Boe did not deserve to be led on only to be let down.

Mike swooped Marcus up and took hold of Petunia's hand. "Let's go."

Chapter 8
S'mores

Marcus was so excited to see Brady Boe and Sasha that he nearly knocked them over. Sasha returned his excitement by picking him up and twirling him around until they both became dizzy and staggered around. The checking out process was fast. Mike along with Petunia gathered everyone up and made their way towards the car. Ms. Suzy Faye called trying to catch up with the Wells pace.

"Excuse me, Mr. and Mrs. Wells."

Mike turned around. Petunia continued to listen to Sasha tell about the crafts she made. Mike got Petunia's attention.

"I don't mean to hold you up," explained Ms. Suzy Faye. "But, I need to inform you of an event that took place last night concerning your daughters."

Mike and Petunia's ears perked up. Brady Boe thought her heart was going to stop for a minute. Mike directed her and the other kids to wait for them by a nearby bench while he and Petunia heard what Ms. Suzy Faye had to say.

"I really don't want to alarm you. The girls were never harmed in any way. Well, they were shaken up for a moment."

Mike looked impatient and started to tell Ms. Suzy Faye to get on with it, but Petunia beat him to it.

"Ms. Suzy Faye, just tell us what happened."

"Well, during the campfire and s'more celebration we convene on the last night, someone was chasing your girls through the woods. We had to file a report, but we have not found out who it was."

Ms. Suzy Faye did not know how to interpret the look she got from each of them.

"Like I said, the girls were not harmed and were quite brave. A few of our male counselors chased whomever it was out to the parking lot. The person jumped in a car and took off. We also disciplined one of our counselors for not being more careful with their safety. I'm really sorry, but we had to let you know."

Petunia took Mike's arm. "Let's go, honey. It's been a long day." Petunia then turned to Ms. Suzy Faye. "Thank you for informing us. When you find out something, please let us know."

"I sure will, Mrs. Wells."

Mike looked at Petunia, "She's gone too far, Petunia."

"I know."

Sasha and Brady Boe could tell their parents were upset. Sasha ran over a hugged them, "I missed you guys."

Mike rubbed her head. "Well, you are going home now, Kiddo."

Brady Boe felt like she failed them. They trusted her to not get into any trouble, and then that crazy night had to happen.

"Brady Boe, are you alright honey?" Asked Petunia.

"I'm sorry about what happened," was all she could say.

Petunia held her close. "I'm just glad you're okay. We can talk more about it later okay?"

Brady Boe nodded and felt a little better.

Before they got into the car to leave, Margie and Terra ran over to say good-bye and give Sasha, Brady Boe, and Taylor a hug.

Brady Boe could tell Margie was going to get all mushy just like Sasha did at different times. She just had that look in her eyes.

"Brady Boe, I had a great time with all of you. Thank you for caring enough to help me be able to come."

It had been an emotional day for Brady Boe she had to fight to keep the tears from forming and falling. Margie was right. She did care enough. Instead of words, she gave Margie another hug and quickly jumped into the car.

On the ride home, Taylor talked about how much she missed her dog and her parents. Sasha pulled out a bracelet she made for Petunia and a penholder she made for Mike. Brady Boe gave Marcus a sucker and a small rubber firefly she bought at the Canteen store. Marcus was super excited and begged for someone to open the sucker while he pretended the firefly was buzzing through the air.

Taylor's parents were anxiously awaiting their arrival. They ran over as they saw the car pulling into the driveway. They showered Taylor with hugs and kisses. Mike wanted to give the girls something to make up for the dreadful night it sounded like they had at camp, so he invited Taylor and her family back for a campfire and s'mores. Petunia winked at him, she knew exactly what he was doing and she loved him for it.

Taylor's parents accepted the invitation and said they would be right back over as soon as Taylor saw her dog and dropped her things off.

Sasha yelled out to Taylor. "Bring your dog back too, Taylor!"

"Alright!" replied Taylor.

In light of all that had happened, Petunia was glad to have her family at home and safe. She instructed Sasha to grab a few more chairs while Mike gathered wood and got the fire started out back. "Brady Boe why don't you come with me to get the s'mores and hot dogs ready to go out."

Brady Boe followed her mom into the kitchen. While Brady Boe was placing items on the tray, Petunia gathered the skewers and drinks.

"Brady Boe, I need to ask you a question."

"Yes, mom."

"I was just wondering how you felt about seeing your birth mom."

Brady Boe felt caught off guard. She never expected that question. She hesitated trying to find the right way to answer the question.

"I just want you to know it's normal to be curious about her, but I don't want you for a second to think anything is wrong with you because you're adopted. Your father and I saw your value from the first day we met you. From day one, we wanted to give you so much."

Brady Boe felt emotional again. It was like Petunia was in her head. The last thing she wanted to do was hurt her parents.

"What is it, Brady Boe?"

"Mommy, I just..."

"Go ahead honey. What is it?"

"I do want to see her. I have questions to ask her."

Petunia felt her heart drop. She knew Brady Boe was curious, but she did not want her to want to see her. "Well, honey sometimes more harm is caused trying to get your answers."

"If you and dad saw I was so special, then why didn't she see it? Why could I just be given away?"

Petunia looked Brady Boe straight in her eyes. "Look, Honey. I can't answer for her. Sometimes people do things thinking they are making the situation better, but sometimes those things haunt you for the rest of your life. I can tell you, the worth she placed on herself at the time she gave you up had nothing to do with your value. You just happened to be the victim of circumstance."

Silence rested in the kitchen. Brady Boe just wanted to let Petunia's words sink in. She did not want to need to see her birth mom, but she did. Brady Boe ran to go get her journal. She wanted to show Petunia the questions she wrote down.

Petunia examined the words on the paper. A tear rolled down her cheek. She wiped it away quickly.

"I made you cry. I don't want to hurt you. I probably don't belong here!"

"Stop now, Brady Boe! That is why I am crying. My tears are because you are hurt. I never wanted that for you. Here you are a gifted child, endowed with so much love and wisdom. I don't want you to miss the opportunity to be aware of what you possess trying to figure out why your birth mom gave you up. One day, you may find your answers, but I hope at that time you handle them with long skewers like those we use with the campfire. They may be needed answers, but they do not define who you are."

Petunia put her arms around Brady Boe and squeezed her tight. Brady Boe promised herself at that moment that she would never hurt Petunia again. Suddenly Sasha charged into the room, "Dad's..."

"What happened? You guys have been crying." Her eyes darted from Petunia to Brady Boe.

"Everything is fine, Sasha," Petunia assured her. "We just had a little chat. It has been quite a day for all of us."

"You're telling me," said Sasha. "That's why we are going to celebrate tonight. Taylor and her parents are out back already, and dad has the fire blazing high!"

"Give me a hug, Sasha," said Petunia. "I love you, Honey."

"I love you too mom. Dad needs you to bring the food." "Come on, Brady Boe. Taylor brought her dog for us to play with!"

Petunia busied herself putting the final additions on the tray. Brady Boe allowed Sasha to lead her to the fun. Though nothing had changed, Brady Boe felt like a large weight had been lifted off her shoulders. She truly loved her family.

Just as Sasha said, the fire was blazing high. The sky was clear, and the air held a hint of coolness in it. It was the perfect summer night to make s'mores. Taylor commented on how much better it was than at camp.

The adults sat around the fire discussing everything from politics to things you could use from your kitchen to clean house. The kids enjoyed running around in the dark with their flashlights while Taylor's dog chased them. Occasionally, they would run over and refuel themselves with s'mores and hot dogs. Marcus stuffed his mouth with marshmallows right out of the bag, while also seeing how many he could burn over the fire. Times like this made Brady Boe wonder why she even questioned her identity.

The night grew late. Marcus was the first to wind down. He climbed onto Mike's lap and yawned. With chocolate and marshmallow smeared around his mouth, he looked like a little animal of some sort, but a sleepy one.

"Dad, I think Marcus is ready for bed," said Sasha pinching his cheeks. Marcus had no strength to squirm from her grasp.

Taylor's parents thanked the Wells for the wonderful time and stated they were going to take Marcus' que and go to bed.

"Mom, can we walk Taylor to her door?" Asked Sasha.

Petunia turned to Mike. "They'll be fine dear."

"Come on, Brady Boe. Let's go!"

Brady Boe and Sasha rushed to follow Taylor and her parents. Before going in the house, Taylor yelled out, "Group hug!"

The three girls hugged until Taylor's parents broke them apart.

"Bye, Taylor," yelled Sasha and Brady Boe as they ran toward home across the street.

"Bye," called Taylor in response.

Sasha stopped Brady Boe right before they reached the back yard.

"Brady Boe, I want to tell you something."

"What is it, Sasha?"

"I'm really sorry for being mad at you at camp."

"Look, Sasha…"

"No, don't say it, Brady Boe. I really am sorry. I'm glad your birth mom didn't keep you because you wouldn't be my sister if she did. Have you ever thought about what your life would have been like with a young mom who didn't want you? You think you're sad now, you would really be sad and probably neglected."

"Wait, Sasha. How do you know so much about this?"

"I was reading this book that I got from the library about this orphan girl who ran away because her mom didn't like her. The mom said she got in the way of her life. So, the book was about all the adventures this girl had."

"What happened to her, Sasha?"

"She found a family that loved her and took her in."

"I think we should hurry inside, Sasha, before mom and dad start worrying."

Sasha had opened another door in Brady Boe's mind. She never thought life could be miserable with her birth mom.

Petunia was cleaning up the leftover s'more fixings when Brady Boe and Sasha walked into the backyard.

"Hey, girls. That was quite an evening. You will have to tell me all about camp tomorrow."

"Oh, Mom. It was fun!" Raved Sasha.

"Did you have fun, Brady Boe?"

"Yes, I guess."

"Well, that doesn't sound encouraging."

"I didn't know Terra was going to be so into Ryan like she was."

"Oh," said Petunia.

"Yeah, I think I have some questions about marshmallows and chocolates."

Petunia looked confused.

"Ms. Suzy Faye told us to keep our marshmallows and chocolate in our own graham cracker," replied Sasha.

"Now, I see," said Petunia. "We should have that talk soon girls."

"Mom, I have one more question."

"Alright, Sasha. One more. Then, we are off to bed."

"Why are s'mores called s'mores?'

"Sasha, really," complained Brady Boe. She knew Sasha would do anything to stall bedtime.

"It's okay, Brady Boe. I think I know the answer." Petunia put together a s'more for demonstration then she began her explanation.

"You see the s'more represent layers of a person. You have the hard graham cracker. That is the barrier. It keeps things from getting in and things from getting out. Once that barrier is broken you expose the soft gooey marshmallows, which is the part people don't always get to see because it's hidden. Sometimes, people feel a little self-conscious about showing that part to others. Next, is the chocolate. It represents sweet freedom. You can only get to it if you remove the other layers though. Some feel it's too dangerous to feel that free, so they keep the other graham cracker on the other side of it in case they need to throw up another barrier."

Quiet seemed to overtake the room after Petunia's explanation.

Brady Boe felt like the words were meant for her. The conversation she had with Petunia in the kitchen and the conversation she had with Sasha on the way back from Taylor's house seem to flood her thoughts at that very moment.

Sasha was amazed that the s'more could be so important. "Wow! I didn't know it meant all that."

"Well, that is my version," said Petunia. Petunia gave them both a kiss on the forehead and ushered them inside.

That night, Brady Boe wrote in her journal.

Dear Journal,

I am starting to believe I have created a fairy tale in my mind about my birth mom. I want to believe that she really loves me... that she just made a mistake. What Sasha said tonight really made me think. I could have been in a bad situation. The problem is, I will never know unless I ask my questions and get answers from the one who knows: my birth mom. Someone is trying to get me. They showed up at camp and scared me to death. I don't know what they want, I keep thinking it is my birth mom trying to get me back. Maybe I should not be afraid and stand up to whoever it is. My mom described me just the way I see myself. I'm a s'more.

Goodnight!

The End

The Anatomy of a S'more

Graham cracker= Hard shell, protective layer.
Marshmallow= Soft, vulnerable, caring.
Chocolate= Sweet wisdom, distinct taste.

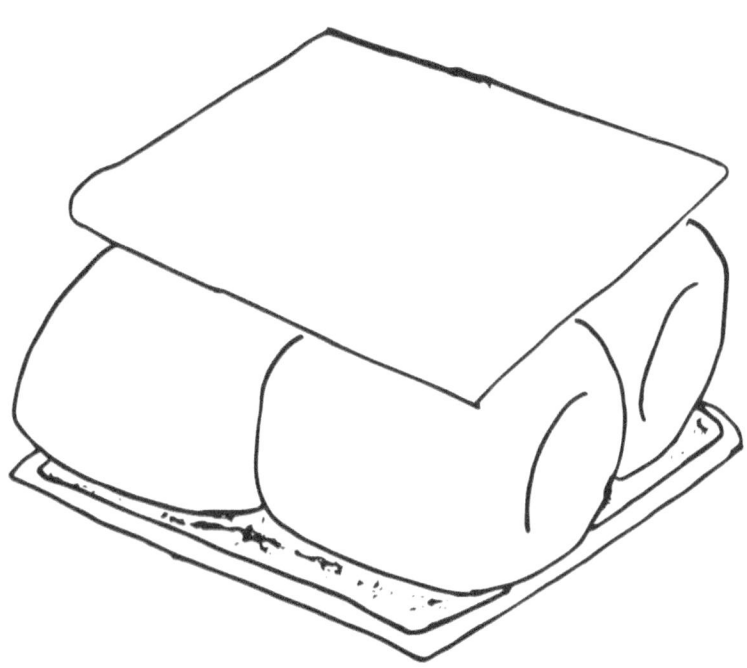

www.ingramcontent.com/pod-product-compliance
Lightning Source LLC
Chambersburg PA
CBHW050832180626
46814CB00004B/1591